LUNA STATION
QUARTERLY

Issue 044 | December 2020

The Circus Issue

Editor-in-Chief
Jennifer Lyn Parsons

Editors
Rocky Breen • Anna Catalano • Linda Codega
Wanda Evans • Angelica Fyfe • Cathrin Hagey
Sarah Pauling • Cait Ryan • Carly Racklin • Shana Ross
Gô Shoemake • Margaret Stewart • Izzy Varju

LUNA STATION PRESS
NEW JERSEY

First Paperback Edition December 2020
ISBN: 978-1-949077-20-9

Luna Station Quarterly publishes short fiction on March 1st, June 1st,
September 1st, and December 1st. For more information and submission
guidelines, please visit our website at lunastationquarterly.com

For Luna Station Press

Creative Director - Tara Quinn Lindsey
Editor-in-Chief & Founder - Jennifer Lyn Parsons

 LUNA STATION PRESS

www.lunastationpress.com

CONTENTS

Editorial

Tara Quinn Lindsey

Tara Quinn Lindsey is a poet & essayist and the Creative Director of Luna Station Press. Her books include *The Esbat Sequence, sQuallor//gLamour, Invisible Compositions* & *Bedtime Stories For Insouciant Alchemists*. To learn more, visit her at taralindsey.com

We really need the circus right now.

From this End-of-2020 vantage point, it could be argued that we need a lot of things right now. Your mileage may vary when it comes to deciding what those things are. But for the sake of simplicity, I return to my original point.

We really need the circus right now.

Why, you might ask? Think for a moment about what the circus provides. Laughter. Wonder. Courage. Beauty. Possibility. Creativity. I could go on, but I think you get my point.

The circus lifts us up. The circus, like the tarot, could be considered a microcosm of the human experience, from Fool to World. If we would just allow ourselves to be simple enough to receive its gifts.

I'm not sure, if I'm being honest, that this issue gets it entirely right. Too many people, even good writers, are stuck in a deconstructionist pose. It's all creepy circuses & dilapidated carnivals & scary clowns. Enough, already!

We did our best to keep them out of here, but many of the submissions we received were suffused with that particular darkness. This is most unfortunate. I'd blame 2020, but I know these opinions about The Theatre of the Fantastique predate this year of division & death.

All I can ask, if you're reading this, is to go to a circus next year, when this is all over. Whether it's a local tent show or the glamour of Cirque du Soleil (if they survive), you should go.

If you bring a child, they'll surely tell you when you should laugh. Better yet, maybe you should go by yourself, so you can drop all poses & preconceptions & allow the very real magick on display to effect you. I promise, you will have more deep & varied emotions than you were expecting. If you are brave enough to let it happen.

Until then, enjoy these stories, and take care of yourselves.

L S Q | 044

Reassured that we do, indeed, have souls

we take our seats at the Mycelial Circus

and wait for the show to begin ...

-Quinn, of Thorn

Silks

Jennifer Lyn Parsons

Jennifer Lyn Parsons is a writer, programmer, and maker. With influences ranging from Laura Ingalls Wilder to Jim Jarmusch, her tales feature a rare physicality with details that feel hand-carved. When not writing code or prose, she is also the editor-in-chief of the venerable Luna Station Quarterly. She finds joy in video games, comics books, discovering music new and old, and making things out of wool, paper, and wood.

"You're so busy doubting yourself while so many others are intimidated by your potential."
- Unknown

***

Anton rubbed his balding head while Jules ranted.

"You're trusting her with a solo act?" The senior aerialist's voice echoed against the excellent acoustics of the theatre. "She's self-taught, she misses details. I have to handle setting up the silks for her half the time."

The ringmaster held up his hand with a sigh. "Enough. You know we struggle to attract an audience. We need fresh acts. She'll handle a solo just fine."

Thalia sat in the balcony, slumped low and hidden from sight. Her gut churned as she listened to the two men. It was her act they were discussing, though she didn't need to eavesdrop to know how Jules felt about her. She and the senior aerialist grated on each other, like oil and water.

Shortly after discussing her shortcomings, the men left the stage. Thalia remained, gnawing on a fingernail as she worked up the desire to stand. Maybe it would be better to just sit here like one of the living statues that handed out roses in front of the theatre to lure folks in for the show. If she stayed perfectly still for long enough, she might even turn to stone, if she was lucky.

***

Everything changed the day Thalia soloed for the first time. It wasn't the applause that did it. It wasn't the clumsy misstep she made on her entrance. It wasn't the crowd's gasp as the anti-grav lifts launched her too far to the left so she almost missed the next silk rope, nearly falling. It wasn't the minor praise from Anton and it definitely wasn't the sneer from Jules after she left the stage.

It was earlier, during rehearsal for a new juggling act, as she slipped onto the balcony to watch. A stranger sat in one of the faux velvet seats, a grin of delight on her face. Thalia crept over to her, unheard over the rehearsing act's soundtrack blaring over the speakers.

She leaned in and whispered in the young woman's ear. "You're in my chair."

A loud yelp focused all eyes in the house on them and Thalia giggled. The performers glared for a moment, then began picking up fallen pins.

"I'm Thalia and you're trespassing. I will call security to throw you out."

The young woman shrugged, smiling. "No you won't, you don't have security."

Thalia gave her a confused look.

"I'm Regine, new stagehand...and security."

***

Regine was rough, strong, bold, and not shy about showing Thalia she was deeply desired. They had napped earlier that afternoon, which had turned into something lovely and passionate, and now they talked.

Thalia sat, tidying her hair. "Anton is barely keeping us from going under. He's might tell us it's the last show any day now."

"It's a sinking ship, love." Regine lay there, playing with the hem of Thalia's blouse. Audition for another show. Maybe a traveling circus? I'll be your assistant."

"That's sweet. It does sound kind of exciting, but...those gigs go to better trained performers than me."

Regine shook her head. "You don't see the audience when you're up there. They love you."

"I..." Thalia started to reply, the contradiction coming easily, but stopped herself. "Let me think about it, okay? Anton gave me my start, a chance when no one else would."

Still shaking her head, Regine's kissed her hand. "You're too loyal for your own good, love."

Thalia nodded. "I know. And you're right. It's a lost cause, but then so were you." She smirked and saw the tension lessen in Regine's shoulders. "I just need to process the idea a little, okay?"

***

It was a challenging rehearsal. Afterward, Thalia hid in the balcony. As she sat having a good cry, the door quietly swooshed open. A moment later Regine was there, flopping into the next seat.

"Don't let Jules get to you," she said as a greeting. "You're special and he resents it."

Thalia shook her head, her nose red and sniffling. "You say that because you love me."

"No," Regine's tone grew more serious. "You're special and that is why I fell for you."

When Thalia didn't smirk at that, Regine asked what happened.

"Jules complained again that he has to help all the time."

Regine's face grew red and she began to stand. "Did he seriously say he had to do your job for you? I'm gonna tell him where he can shove his damn training."

Thalia put a hand on her arm. "Reggie. It's okay. He's kind of right. I do need some help. I have to work harder, build better foundations."

"It's not okay. Anton needs to protect you better. You're too good for that shit." Regine allowed herself to be pulled back down.

Thalia nodded, "It's a long shot, but I...am applying to Elysium Bazaar tomorrow."

***

An aerialist. It was all Thalia ever wanted to be. Flying through the air, swinging and twisting between the lengths of silk, then leaping into the void as the anti-grav units buoyed her to the next set of silks. It was terrifying and exhilarating and worth every hour of work she had put into learning the art.

There hadn't been any support in getting there. No money for the training and definitely no funds for the costly investment of a place with the equipment and space to practice on her own. So she saved and managed to get the basic silks now mounted to her apartment's ceiling. She went to every circus in the surrounding ten sectors of Torant City and took notes. She practiced until her hands were calloused and her arms strong.

She didn't know the name of any pose when she joined Anton's Circus of Dreams but she had earned a place there and her skills grew quickly. Now it seemed that time was coming to a close and the future was uncertain.

Yet the silks were still there for her. Anchored yet flexible, they still had much to teach her, and she was a willing student.

***

Lights flooded the theatre. From the stage to the high rafters, it glittered off the fine filaments woven into the silks. The fabric swayed as Thalia pulled herself up, anti-gravs carrying her higher and higher. She stopped two-thirds up their length and began her dance.

Regine had kissed her soundly before she entered the stage, now very far below. "You've got this," she whispered. The aerialist's nerves were wound tight tonight, there was a ring master in the audience. An opening at Elysium Bazaar was available and they were scouting her, much to Anton's disappointment.

Thalia moved across the silks. Arabesque, split, side lean, swing and then a leap to the next set of silks while the crowd gasped. It felt good, until it didn't. The anti-grav sputtered off and there was not a sound in the theatre as Thalia barely grasped the next silk and swung there for a moment, shaking. Anton started to step onto the stage, but she waved him off.

A deep breath later, she began improvising. She did drops and roll ups and things she only tried in her apartment, abandoning choreography. She failed the audition, but she would finish her act for the audience.

***

It was no surprise that the ring master for Elysium Bazaar did not come back stage. Thalia had missed something in her setup on the anti-gravs, some detail she had forgotten to check.

She told everyone, Regine included, that she wanted to be on her own for a bit. Donning street clothes, she left by the stage door, intent on finding a quiet space to think. A few blocks away was an observation deck looking out across Torant City.

"This far from the Lowers it almost looks beautiful," she thought, surfacing old memories of more vulnerable times.

"Ye've come a long ol' way, dearie. I seen ye. Been watchin' yer shows."

Thalia had not heard the old woman approach yet somehow was not startled by her appearance.

She patted Thalia's arm. "Jus ye wait an' see. Ye've worked hard. Ye'll get yer due."

"Th...thank you, Grannie," Thalia stuttered out, hoping the spontaneous endearment didn't insult her.

The old woman nodded, smiling as she turned and toddled off.

A sense of calm washed over Thalia. Something about the old

woman's validation had bolstered Regine's reassurances. She wasn't sure how it would happen, but Thalia was ready for whatever came next.

***

"Someone left a note," a stagehand called to Thalia as she opened her dressing room door, garment bag over her shoulder.

She nodded, entering the closet-sized room with the massive mirror. An envelope sat in the only clear spot on her table of makeup and brushes. She placed the bag on the chair, then slit the envelope open with a hair pin.

Turn off the machines and play. Then come see me. Teach us your style, if you are willing. We leave next week. - MV

Madame Velena. She ran Cirque Paradisio, which was getting astounding reviews, and audiences. They were new, but were already taking apprentices. They wanted her in a senior role. Thalia's heart soared.

That night, high above the stage, she signaled to Regine to turn off the anti-gravs. She had no plan, but her body knew what would excite wonder and awe in the hearts of the audience below. She trusted her hours of practice, she trusted her instincts, and she trusted her heart. For the first time, everything felt right and her heart was full.

As she left the stage to wild applause, she saw Madame Velena take her leave with a smile on her face.

***

"This is your suite." Madame Velena opened the door into a brightly-lit space. Dressing area to one side, silks mounted to the ceiling on the other and a door across from them that led to her private quarters. It was close but cozy.

"Costumes in that closet. The rest of your things in there." Velena indicated the bedroom. "One of the troupe will be around to give you a tour of the ship and ensure you have all you need."

"Thank you," Thalia answered, doing her best not to gape at the space.

"No, Thalia, thank you." Velena smiled at her. "We need creativity and energy and honestly we need true artists. Audiences grow weary of perfect form. They want grit within the grace."

The lump in her throat left Thalia speechless. With a nod, Velena squeezed Thalia's arm as she left.

Regine would arrive soon to say goodbye for the next few months. Thalia's tears would flow freely then. For now, there was a set of silks here in her new room that she wanted to test. Heart full of gratitude and renewed confidence, she began to play with ideas for her what felt like her true first performance.

Margins

Elizabeth Hinckley

As a naturalist and an author, Elizabeth Hinckley has a passion for both the natural world and the power of story, and their ability to inspire the human spirit. She is the author of David, A Rat. She lives in New Jersey, home to a surprisingly beautiful and diverse array of natural wonders, which she explores frequently.

It was the height of a blazing hot summer day and Adrian felt the heat baking him as he slowly walked across the expanse of empty parking lot in the furthest corner of the mall complex. Behind him, the Big Top rose like a confection against a sapphire sky, all scalloped edges and cotton candy colors, magnificent and magical. Ahead, a low guardrail sat under a curtain of still-spring-green maples and willows, and in between, a dark green that promised thick, cool forest over water. Ever since he was a small child, he had always been drawn to the edges of things— the places just out of sight of most. He could always tell these sorts of places from a distance—nature that was pushed off to the margins of developed land, places where streams had to be, because water had to be *somewhere*, if you had civilized all of the places it would have liked to be. He couldn't understand why so many people never seemed to be as interested in such places, the places on the edge of life, where all the interesting and best things happened.

When he was small, he would find places like this, playing in the woods for hours, balancing on tree branches high above streams. Usually alone, once his friends had adopted their parents' terror of ticks and pedophiles who they imagined inhabited the woods. There was a little girl friend of his for a time who seemed to share this understanding, but when they got to be around 12 or so, her parents became more protective. There was a point where it occurred to him suddenly that it was childish to ask if she wanted to play, so he changed his wording to 'hang out in the woods.' Whether it was a newly frosty reception from her mother, or an evasive deferral from the girl, their rebuffs caused him, forlornly, to stop looking for her company after a while. He simply returned to the shelter of the woods, this time in solitude, to enjoy its shelter, its beauty, and mystery.

But when it wasn't the school year, when he lived with his mother, he spent the summer with his father and his circus family. His uncles and aunts and his cousins, his grandparents and all of the people in the show and crew—these were the people who understood life on the margins. Once, in social studies, there was a chapter in their textbook called "Life on the Margins." He was low-key excited about reading it for homework, thinking it would be about interesting people doing things out of the ordinary. Instead, it was all about people who were poor, displaced, or disenfranchised. He always thought of his circus family and his summer life as being on the margins—where all of the excitement, beauty, and magic were. Things he thought didn't exist if you only stayed where it was safe and neat and predictable, like the baking hot mall parking lot. As he drew nearer to the mysterious promise of the cool woods, he was alive with the vitality of his summer life: where he worked out in the morning, explored in the afternoon, and performed at night—and where, even though they lived in trailers and never stayed anywhere too long, he felt the most at home.

He was an extremely athletic youth, necessary for being a performing acrobat with his family, the Majestic Majerniks. He could endure hours of disciplined, backbreaking workouts in the heat without complaint, but that did not mean he was immune to the sweet relief of walking into the shade at the edge of the parking lot, so dramatic it was like drinking the cool juice that might come from a flower as beautiful as the tiger lilies lining the edge of the woods. There was something about tiger lilies that stirred his soul; perhaps it was because they bloomed in June and, every year, that was when he rejoined the circus and his happiest times returned.

This summer was an important one and every joy was both amplified and bittersweet. He would be turning 18 this year, and had to make a choice—one of which might mean the last of times like these. On the one hand, he would have to decide whether to go to college and choose a career. Any career, he supposed, so there were a variety of possibly good futures to consider, but for what college would cost, he realized that whatever he chose, he would have to stick with it.

The other option was to join his family's act, which would mean not just summers, but a lifetime of traveling to where the work was. He loved it and thought that's what he might like to do, but sometimes he could hear his mother's thoughts in the back of his head—thoughts that told him there was no stability in that life. He was still a teenager and did his share of pretending not to listen to parental advice, especially becoming defensive of his paternal family when Mom started sounding just a little bitter, but an astute observer might note that the strength of his defensiveness gave him away—that her concerns had lodged themselves in his mind enough to become, just a little bit, his own.

The nature of their work was risk-taking, of pushing oneself to the next level, so he did not like to think of himself as taking the safer path. There was nothing like the feeling of being completely, fully present because your safety, or life, or someone else's, depended on it. Everything felt so focused and clear up on the high wire, and he was prouder of his work there than anything else he did in life.

If he really thought of it, part of him wondered if, by committing to it permanently, would he grow tired of it? This frightened him the most.

Summer was magical, his happiest time. Part of him worried that growing up meant that the magic of his boyhood summers would fade, like having Christmas every day. He was disciplined enough to withstand the hard work and boredom of some other career, if he could return to the circus to dream. But if the circus lost its magic to him, he would regret it all of his life. Although he didn't want to admit she might be right, his mother's practical concerns became an option he gnawed on when distracted by his future.

Fortunately, he did not have much time to gnaw. His father was excited to have him back for the summer, and worked him into the act. As the weeks went by, Adrian would build back up his strength and skills, and by the end of summer, would increase his role in the show, but he'd have to earn it. Adrian knew that his father would love to have him join them next year for good, but tried not to show it. Adrian thought his father did not want to cause trouble with Mom, who already held plenty of resentment over their relationship and his upbringing. To Mom, it was always "that itinerant life", or "that circus". She liked to use the word "scrounging" when the subject came up. As Adrian got older and resented the attack on that part of his life, there had been a time a few years ago when he had become adversarial with his mother, and his father surprisingly reproached him.

They were walking through the dust of the center ring as Adrian complained about her, when his father stopped and said, "I would not have you disrespect your mother, son", in his Old-World sort of way of speaking.

"But Otecko, all she ever does is disrespect our life!"

Serj sighed, and sat down on the ring wall, motioning Adrian to sit with him.

"Son, you are more like me than you are like your mother. It seems self-serving to say so, but it is the truth. And that is why she fears to lose you."

"But, she won in the divorce, and she got me. And all she seems to be trying to do is to take more, make me turn on our life."

"No one won the divorce. It is not a game of football. And if one knows who one is, then there is no reason to get mad when someone doesn't like the way you live." And pausing, he gently added, " I don't think it's so much *our* life...as it is *my* life. Your life is your own, and you are still deciding."

Adrian opened his mouth to protest, but he knew his Otecko's body language all too well—when you work so closely together, you can read each other without words. So he knew he didn't have to defend anything, but closed his mouth and let his father continue.

"When I first saw your mother, she came to the show." Serj let a mischievous, wistful smile escape as he spoke. "She was with her boyfriend...but I liked her, what can I say? She had a nice smile and she did not seem too happy with him, so I ran to the audience and held out a flower—and when she reached for it, I pulled it back and shook my finger 'no, no, no!'" He smiled at the memory.

"Oh, that boyfriend, *Tom*," punctuating the air with his finger as he said it, "...was not too happy. So I grabbed his hand and shook it and everybody laughed. And I took the rose between my teeth, climbed the pole, and did my whole act for her. And when I grabbed the ceiling rope to come down, I swung it till it reached up the aisle and I hopped off right next to her and gave her the rose."

Adrian smiled, imagining his parents happy together. "So that's how you got together?"

"Oh, no. That Tom was in the way. But I looked for her in the lobby after, for the pictures with the fans, and she dragged Tom over for a picture. I pretended to not have good English and said, 'Oh, come for autograph! What your name is?' He says, you go ahead, and so we talked for a minute alone. I wrote my email on the back of the autograph and asked her to write to me, 'to be pen pal, no?' And she did!"

"At first she pretended just to be friendly, but as we wrote back and forth, I thought she liked me too. Then one day, she said she never bought my broken English act one bit, and she knew what I was up to."

"I said 'what about Tom?' And she told me that he was a stable guy with a solid future, and that I was great but he was the better bet."

"Ouch! So what did you do?"

"We had a Philly show coming up so I told her to come. She did. Then the next was New York and it was only a little further, so I asked her to come for a nice time in the city, before we moved on and I wouldn't see her for a while. And when she went home on Christmas break, we had a few weeks off so I got on the train and rode all the way up to see her."

"From where?"

"From Florida."

"From FLORIDA?! What did Tom say?"

"Oh, he was *nastvany*," (Adrian liked the comfort of Slovak swear words), "but your mother kept him in line by acting like we were just good friends."

He seemed a little sad, as he continued, "She was not trying to be mean, she really wasn't. I think it was more like she was trying to make up her mind." His face opened up kindly. "Like you. So I don't want you to rush."

"So what happened?" Adrian asked, more interested in the story than the question.

"I declared my love for her and asked her to run away and join the circus."

"Ooooh, for real, Otecko?" Adrian grimaced. "Recipe for disaster."

"Not for the right person. I thought I could sweep her off her feet, but looking back, I guess she was just feeling a bit trapped, and wanted to break free. From Tom, from expectations, from...I don't know. But I was young enough to think it was for me, and that the romance of the circus would help."

"But it didn't."

"No. It did not."

They sat for a while.

"So we got married, and we found places for her, to run the food booth or sell souvenirs, and give her a chance to see if she had a knack for any of the arts. She didn't have to, as long as she could contribute something useful. She worked on costumes for a while but got tired of that. Then she did ticket sales, and then she got pregnant with you."

Adrian could barely remember his mother being around the circus, but he had a few memories, being held on her hip and feeling the scratchiness of the sequins on her outfit. It seemed impossible, but he remembered her feeling of restlessness, of impatience. Not in a way of literally remembering her expressing that feeling, but actually feeling it, drinking it in as if drinking milk from the breast. A way of feeling that perhaps all children can feel, and forget as they start to root themselves in their own identities.

"Otecko, why are you telling me all this?"

"Because I love you. And you're the only thing I love more than the circus, so this is important. I want you to have a good life. I think this is a good life, but if you do not love it it will become hard. It must never be just another job. You have to tell a story of who you are, a personal story that means something, whenever you perform. You must be present in the moment, like a monk, but also grow and challenge yourself. Then you will always find the joy and beauty. But if all you need is just enough fantasy to keep you going, you depend on it to solve problems it cannot solve. Instead of growing, you get disappointed in the fantasy. You grow tired of it, like your mother did."

"It sounds pretty obvious what I should do, then."

"Does it?"

"Yeah...how could I choose a coward's way after that sort of speech? A sad kind of life where you sell out and don't shoot for something wonderful?"

Inside his heart, Serj was glad to hear his son's disposition leaned toward a life with him, but he remembered his wife and how something beautiful had gone so wrong. He really had loved her, but wondered if she ever really loved him, the way it had turned out. He was determined that Adrian would not just follow him instead of his own heart. It hadn't worked out before.

"You misunderstand me, son. Think of the people we perform for. They come for a bit of magic. Most of them are not performers, they are regular people. Do we hold them in contempt for having a regular job, for having other sorts of dreams?

There are all kinds of people in the world. Sometimes, they need just a little fantasy, and sometimes we are fortunate enough to give it to someone who never had it at all. And mostly, we give them truth in disguise, which is most beautiful of all. We make the world better. But you have to be the kind of person who sees magic *all* the time to be able to share it with others.

You love the circus now because it has always meant good times for you growing up..."

Adrian tried to interject; it meant so much more to him. Family, pride, his sense of home! But Serj continued, determined to make sure his words reached his son to the bone.

"But you will have to find what it means to you now." He turned and looked his son directly in the eye. "Think about what you need to say with your art. Something you can believe in."

Now, confident that he had said his piece, he relaxed, letting it all go for Adrian to ponder. Then he chuckled and said, "And if you don't have anything to say, you can go get rich as a businessman and take care of me in my old age. I will love you still."

Adrian hopped the guardrail, and his skin stopped baking

instantly under the shade, though the sweat continued to come. The smell of humidity mingled with the earthy scents of the undergrowth, scents that were both sweet and pungent at the same time. He pushed leaves aside as he moved down the embankment, watching for poison ivy. There was a polluted little stream at the bottom, as he would expect from a stream encircling a mall parking lot. Runoff brought litter and oil from the pavement with each rainstorm, so it did not bring the type of wilderness experience one thinks of as natural, when one has little connection to nature in the first place and hungers for untouched places; but to Adrian, a stream was a stream. It still brought life to the creatures that drank from it, and grew alongside it, and despite the litter, it was clear and little fish still swam in small pools outside of the current. They didn't have the luxury to define nature, and so to them, it was their world. Adrian was much the same, and needed water and trees and air to survive, and sought it out wherever he could find it. He deftly clambered across a fallen log—a little too high over the stream for an average person, but a piece of cake for a professional acrobat—and walked deeper into the woods.

The birds were quiet under the canopy. The work of finding a mate was over, and for some, so was the work of raising a brood, so the frenetic singing of spring was no longer so urgent in the languid heat of summer. There was a peacefulness in hearing the animals rest and the plants breathe and grow, and he was certain little eyes must be watching him, properly mindful of his presence if necessary, but unconcerned and unwilling to move. He knew if he were to sit still for a few minutes, perhaps he would spot such eyes, belonging to a toad or a chipmunk, should they decide to shift their hiding space, or retrieve a tasty seed. Maybe even a fawn, lying completely still and scentless in a thicket, sleeping away a few hours while its mother fed on nourishing grass somewhere in the open.

Under the cover of the forest, and now far from the mall, he delighted in the animal feeling of being attentive to scent, to the sights of natural patterns, the small sounds that indicated life. Out here, a snapped twig meant an animal moving; even the sounds of a seed pod bursting could be heard as if it were a tiny localized rain shower. But most exciting of all was the sight that greeted him as he walked into a clearing: a beautiful ring of mushrooms on the forest floor. It was more than a little magical to find a fairy ring, just for itself, but coming from a European family, finding mushrooms was something that had always been part of his life. He'd never actually known anyone outside his family to have even been aware of this thing he didn't have a name for—perhaps it could be termed mushrooming culture, or a food foraging thing—but any of his Majernik relatives had a working knowledge of, and excitement for how to find morels, chanterelles, porcinis, and tons of other delicious fungi. Like him, they were prone to wander into woods wherever they set up, and would make fantastic meals with their finds, even medicines from old family recipes. Though America has its share of passionate mycological hobbyists, they are members of a rare and odd breed, and Adrian had never heard of any; while in many places in Europe, gathering wild edibles is as common as apple picking.

He admired the beauty of the ring—it was about 10 feet across, and while he was curious to identify whether they would be good to eat (or alternatively, highly toxic), he wanted to just look at it, and imagine the kind of feeling he might feel if there really were fairies. In yet another way that he lived on the margins, he was aware that this wasn't something that most other American boys his age did, but he had a great capacity for imagination and fantasy that was precious to him, and which he kept to himself, a product of a life where dreams sustained him and made him somewhat other. In the deep quiet of the woods, he could pretend, just like when he was a little boy, that he had found a magical place between the worlds. Just like the moment when you start to fall asleep and think you are awake but are slipping away, it was a little mysterious, a little dangerous. It was like standing too close to the edge of a great height and half enjoying the terrified feeling of looking down. His natural flair for the dramatic and his robust imagination had eliminated the need to try drugs, but he rolled his eyes back, imagining that's what it might feel like. He took a few steps forward into the ring, and then he fell.

Face planted ungraciously on the ground, reverie broken, he looked up and wondered how he had fallen. There was no log to trip over, and he hadn't kicked anything anyway. He was a professional acrobat—he was not prone to falling. But he was feeling cooler, more so than if the sun had just ducked behind a cloud, and wondered if he had hit his head. And then a great gush of water splashed onto his head, as if some one had poured a drink on him, or thrown a water balloon. All around him, great masses of water splatted one at a time, pockmarking the earth— a volleyball rain of huge drops, and most unpleasant. Rather than be pelted by buckets, he ran for some shelter, through what appeared to be reeds reaching above his head that he hadn't remembered seeing, until he reached a huge white mushroom that towered over him.

He marveled at it for a moment, mind on high alert, then was pummeled once more in the face with a rain splat.

Sheltering under the canopy of the mushroom, the vibration of each rain drop—or rain bucket—shook loose a rain of spores from the gills, showering him with a cinnamon coating that stuck to his wet body, smelling of dust and earth. None too clean, he was nevertheless out of the rain, and finally took a look around.

Giant mushroom. Giant rain. Giant grasses. Suddenly cool, not just because of the rain, but like it was another season entirely. And a twilight sky, even behind the rainstorm.

"And no, I did not fall. I am sure of it," he told himself. He never experienced a moment of unconsciousness, nor the ill feeling of coming back from it. He felt perfectly fine. Instead, he thought back to what he had been thinking of just before he stepped into the faerie ring, and realized that maybe he really did find one heck of a margin. Most people don't see what they're not looking for, but a seeker? Sometimes that's a different story, and Adrian was always looking at the edge of things. As his mind spun, he wondered if...had he really...?

And then, high above him, a sweet voice gently called, "Hello."

***

Adrian looked up and saw the most beautiful girl he had ever seen. She perched elegantly on a low branch of a nearby bush, shaded by the leaves above her chestnut brown hair, as if she had been reading a book, or daydreaming, when the storm broke. Her eyes were ethereal; curious, kind, and somewhat far-away, or at least that's what he felt. And she wore what could only be called raiment—a material so fine that it caught the light and reflected subtle changes in color, like the iridescence of a beetle, or the wing of a grackle. He couldn't even describe what color it was, except that it was no color, or the color of water, except when the sun would bring out rainbow shades for a tiny second as the slightest movement shifted the surface. As beautiful as this would be all on its own, the dress was covered in butterfly wings, as a wedding dress would be covered in lace—cascades of wings overlapping each other and dripping beautiful patterns down the full skirt, so long that wisps of the dress hung down past her dainty feet. He'd never seen a garment so incredibly beautiful, and he worked in the circus.

"Hello." He replied back, almost speechless. What could he say? He supposed he could ask how she had gotten up there, but he suddenly found himself fighting to shout a warning that strangled in his throat, as a huge spider started skittering toward the beautiful girl. It was horrifying, like nothing he'd ever seen. Its massive body was bulbous and glassine, and he was shocked to see right through its body as if looking through a bubble, the iridescent rainbow colors swirling on its surface. Terror chilled his blood as the spider reacher her far faster than he could shout, and fear for her made his knees weak and his stomach drop. It was large enough to ride, a fact that would become pertinent in just a moment, for as the beast approached her, she reached up her hand to pat its head and whisper to it. The creature seemed to lean into her hand, and twitched a few legs lazily in plea-sure. Then she reached under to the narrow spot between its head and body and pulled. A thick ribbon came undone, and something slid off the top of its body as it turned to skitter away. Even though it fell from up in a branch, the item did not thud harshly, but fell softly as if a block of foam. As Adrian wondered what had just happened, his first question was answered. She unfolded a set of delicate wings which lifted her off the branch, and gracefully set her down on the forest floor. Picking up the item, she held it over her head to protect herself from the rain, then flitted over on her little bare feet to where he stood, under the mushroom. She then placed what had been protecting her head on the ground—a cunning little saddle, soft and light and velvety, made from a single dried mushroom.

She appraised him, a knowing smile at the corners of her mouth. "Hello, boy. What is your name?" The way she said it did not feel rude. It was more like she was addressing a creature who she did not know, like a cat lady holding out a dish of food and saying, "Here, kitty." It was disarming and amusing to Adrian, who wondered if it might shock her if he actually spoke back.

He replied, and then she said, "You must come from the human world, do you not?"

He nodded.

Then he asked, "Who are you? What place is this?" It caught her off guard.

She replied with gentle dignity, "In this world, we are not accustomed to humans speaking without first being spoken to." She said it in a way that seemed like she was not angry, but doing him a favor, like she was giving him a bit of coaching.

He was mildly taken aback, but he did not want to offend such a lovely person, someone who was perhaps royalty or high status at least. Though he was almost entirely American in most ways, his father's family had instilled in him a European sense of formality and a performer's courtesy to the audience. Instead of protesting, or even apologizing, he place his hand over his heart, and slightly bowed his head by way of apology. This appeased her instantly.

"Though I do not expect you would have any way of knowing this. It would be more sensible if we could talk freely. Just remember, if you meet anyone else." She paused, still formal, and said, "I am Caoimhe."

"Kee-vah", the sound washed over him like a soft breeze. It sounded strong and soft and beautiful at the same time. Did everything she did or said have some magical way of subtly intoxicating him? It was as if he had never really known beauty before, and not just in the guise of a beautiful-looking person, but also something deeper. Emotion, perhaps, or a sort of knowing. It felt as if pure spirit flowed from her and manifested in ways he could detect, like her scent or the sound of her voice, or the very spirit contained in the sound of her name.

"We don't see many people from your world. In fact, you are the first I've met. This is Tir na nOg".

He replied that he was honored to be her guest, but said nothing more. There followed an extended pause, as Caoimhe looked him over expectantly, before finally realizing that he was holding back. If he were to open up, she'd have to let him know she really meant him to relax. Noting how filthy he now was, it occurred to her that he could not possibly feel on even footing in such a state. She said, "Come. Let us tend to your dignity," she laughed as she grasped his hand. The touch was electric.

The rain burst had stopped, and the air was pleasantly fresh. His clothes, his hair, every surface was caked with wet mushroom spores, but the few that had fallen on Caoimhe fluttered away from her body like glitter, not daring to spoil her beauty. She led him to a pool that had formed between the huge, gnarly roots of a giant tree. Taking in the scope of this new world, he started to make the calculations and realized that in his own they would be quite tiny—a puddle was now a pool, a grass as tall as a tree, and a spider could be ridden.

As he stood at the edge of the pool, he became aware that she was waiting for something. Seeing that he didn't understand, she prompted him with a helpful tone, "You may bathe now."

This he did not expect, but there was no mischief in her approach. She sat herself down on a large rock, tucking her wings down and hugging her knees casually. She appeared completely at ease, like a little bird about to commence preening its feathers. With horror, he realized she really meant it. No, not even just meant it, but sincerely was making a formal offering that she meant magnanimously.

This was not the time to act like a child, he told himself. But undressing in front of her was too much. His clothes were filthy—perhaps he could pass off that he meant to wash the dirt off of everything? He jumped in fully clothed, and resurfaced shaking off the water from his hair with a grin, pleased with the elegant solution.

She laughed, and the sound delighted him. "Do people in your world always bathe with their clothes on?"

"Well, my clothes are just as dirty as I am. They needed a washing," he said, treading water.

"Yes," she said patiently, considering that maybe humans did not know these things, "But it would be cleaner if you took them off and swirled them around in the water. Like this." She made a swirling, rubbing gesture with her hands.

Under the cover of the water, he did so to please her. But with a pile of wet clothes in his arms, he did not know what to do next.

She waited for him patiently, raising her closed eyes to the dappled sunlight streaming through the leaves. She wondered why he did not hang his clothes up on a branch to dry. He had jumped in with them on, and at first she thought he did not know how to wash. Did a servant usually do this for him? She was no servant, and would not do it. Or was it the opposite, and he was a barbarian who did not wash? He did not seem a fool; in fact he was quite deferential. Contemplating him, she realized she did not actually know anything about him at all. It was time to ask.

"Why do you not hang up your clothes?"

Dreading this moment, he found the right words on his tongue just before speaking. "In my world, it is improper to show myself unclothed before a lady."

"Really?" She replied, with genuine puzzlement. Pondering this, she spoke "How then, do you share in the pleasures of the flesh, or make children?"

If he had had a sip of a drink in his mouth, this would be the moment when he spat it out. But once again, there was absolutely no guile in her question, no sense of indiscretion. She really wanted to know.

"Well, of course we do that," he stammered, "but we only take our clothes off when we mean to do that." Jesus, did she mean to do that with him? He blushed fiercely.

But she continued, "Well, if you only take them off for sensual pleasures, then how do you keep your clothes clean?"

Relieved somewhat, he allowed himself to be amused by the conversation. He explained that of course, they removed their clothes for washing, but not in front of other people. They discussed little absurdities in the differences between how their people did things, and as the barriers fell between them, he emerged from the water, finally less self-conscious, and hung his clothes on a branch. He then sat, naked, on a rock across from her, with only the modesty of hugging his knees casually, the way she was.

"You are doing quite well. If I had to live by the rules of your people, I would understand that you would be shy. I don't know why. You are so very beautiful."

Adrian blushed, feeling warm all over. This was a statement of truth, not flattery. In a magical world where beauty surrounded and flowed around him, to be called beautiful made him feel strong and alive, sacred.

Time seemed to stop for them that afternoon. Adrian never had a moment of wondering how they could talk and talk, and never run out of things to say, but found that one thread of conversation opened up to another, and yet another. She told of the faerie court where she lived, and though she had thought the rules of Adrian's human world seemed restrictive, he was fascinated by the arcane ways of the court, which seemed like a complicated game.

She listened, enraptured, as he talked of his life. He was so open, so guileless, like a flower. She knew without asking that he was a being who loved whatever he loved with his whole heart.

And he witnessed, throughout the afternoon, how Caoimhe seemed like the force behind the living web of life around her. Creatures came by frequently, often engaging in some sort of mystical exchange; perhaps an affectionate gesture, a gift of a berry clutched in little mandibles, or to receive some bit of life energy from her aura.

Being around her, he felt alive as if made of sunshine and wind. He didn't feel as if he liked her just because of all of the fantastic things around her, like tame creatures or enchanted sunlight, but because she was made of the stuff that made these things. Her soul was the animating force running through, and connected to, all of them. He felt a part of all of this, that he mattered just by being, and by being near her, too.

It was strange for him to discover that she was old, very old, but the more they talked it felt as if she was forever young at the same time. Like most young people, she had her own ways of doing things. She felt the same chafing against doing things the way she was being told to do them, mixed with the insecurity that she was still too young to challenge those older and wiser.

Though they were alive with the afternoon's idyll, Caoimhe was aware of the flexibility of time in her world, slowly realizing that the precious time they were spending together was running out. The brightness and vitality that shone from Adrian, so fresh and gentle, so open, was starting to fade from her perception; if he spent much more time here, he would start to starve to death before he realized it. She was sad to see him cover his lovely nakedness, but she did not begrudge him trying to fight off the chill he felt as his life energy slowly weakened. She knew that soon, he would have to stay—or he would have to go.

Adrian was distracted by a turtle that had wandered into the clearing, foraging slowly for insects like a cow grazing. "That's Manna," she said, as he contemplated a creature that, to him, was much larger than even a Galapagos tortoise. He had never really studied a turtle up close, and was fascinated by the beautiful patterns in its thick, leathery skin, and the wise look in its deep red eyes. "Would you like to ride him?" she asked.

He laughed, mildly confused but amused all the same. "Sure. But...why? He can't go very fast, to be honest."

"That's not why you would ride him," she said with mild reproach. He would have happily given it a try for any reason, but he sensed a deeper purpose. "You do it to get close to him—to understand him better." She approached the huge beast, and he raised his head to her. She patted his hard, bony head and he closed his eyes in contentment. "He says he would like to show us his world."

They both climbed up onto Manna's shell, and she told him to lie down. Opening her wings carefully across her back, she laid down next to him, and the edges of her wing tickled the side of his arm. Manna had been basking in the sun, and his smooth, bony shell radiated warmth that soaked into them. They looked up into the canopy of the forest as the patterns of light through the leaves slowly changed with Manna's crawling pace. Sometimes he stopped to eat something he found, but standing or moving, everything was gentle and slow and deliberate. Lying there with her, Adrian felt like he could understand something new about the world, about time moving differently.

She asked him about the kinds of things he did in his world. He didn't think she meant school or a job, but the things that made him who he was. "It may sound strange, but I walk..." trying to find the words to explain the circus to her, "...I perform dangerous feats in a show for people."

"Oh yes, we have performers. Singers and dancers, actors and such. What makes it dangerous?"

"Well, I walk on a rope high above the ground. If you fall, you'll get hurt or die, so it takes a lot of concentration."

"Why do you do things that are dangerous?"

"Well, it takes a lot of skill, and the danger makes you really good—you have to be perfect every time."

"Why not do something with skill that's not dangerous? Don't you have things like that?"

Turning towards her, he thought about it. It was something he knew in his heart, something he felt, but now that he was explaining it, he couldn't quite find the words.

"Yes, of course we do—we've got musicians and people who make you laugh, or do things that are hard but not dangerous.

But...sometimes, when you're up there doing something amazing, it makes people feel like they can believe in amazing things."

"But mostly, when I'm up there, and I have to do something perfectly or die, it makes me do things better than I ever did them before. I can't think of anything else but the thing in front of me, and then everything makes sense in the purest way." A few moments passed with the gentle plodding motion of Manna. "Like now," he added quietly. She looked him in the eye, and just as he had learned to understand what Manna felt like, she suddenly understood him, too.

Neither would have broken the spell between them just yet, but it was broken for them.

"What have you found, Little Sister?" A voice cooed from above, its sweetness disguising a predatory intent. Startled, Manna pulled inside his shell, and the sudden movement slid them off his back. Caoimhe, stricken, met Adrian's eyes, transmitting danger. A rabbit has no defense against the weapons of tooth and claw, but its magic lies in stilling its motion, in becoming invisible. Adrian wasn't quite invisible, but he knew to be still and silent, to let Caoimhe divert the attention of the newcomer.

The faery Aoife was more resplendent and glorious than even her sister, dripping with the trappings of courtly status, to the point where she seemed weighed down by an abundance of pearls, shells, feathers, and silvery threads of gossamer. He disliked her instantly.

"Oh, just a sweet creature I found to play with. I was about to send him back to his world," she said lightly. But the bond between Adrian and Caoimhe was so strong now that he felt her heart: she was protecting him.

"But why? Is it amusing? You must take care with your creatures—look, it's starving! Let's offer it something to eat," she said maliciously.

"No!" Caoimhe replied, a little too forcefully. But Aoife read her intent easily. 'Little sister had formed an attachment? This could be fun,' she thought.

Caoimhe did not hate her sister and her petty ways, and in fact, was a little in awe of her. But she knew to fear her capricious whims. So many times, Aoife had gotten the best of Caoimhe, and knew how to manipulate her. Yet after making a fool of her, Aoife would claim that it was for her own good. That in place of their lost mother, it was her responsibility to teach her sister how to survive the intrigues of the court, and if her methods were sometimes cruel, they were all the more effective. It was a web that Caoimhe had not yet learned to navigate successfully.

"You there, creature. Human?" she demanded, as if trying to discern an unfamiliar flavor from a trifle. He paused, looking surreptitiously towards Caoimhe for guidance, but she was silent. She knew she would have to be aloof, and he would have to use his wits, to slip this confrontation. "Speak!"

Caoimhe gave the slightest nod while her sister's gaze focused on him. "I am, my Lady," as he bowed. This seemed to please her somewhat, and she said, "How curious. It seems to know its manners. Do you like it?"

"He's harmless. I was about to let him go..." Caoimhe replied, as if she didn't care.

"Well, perhaps I'll keep him, then." Caoimhe's eyes widened, to Aoife's quiet delight. She turned to Adrian and said, "Here, pet. Come sit and have something to eat." She whistled, and a moment later, a robin appeared with a worm in its mouth. She dropped it in front of Adrian, where it wiggled, larger than a snake at his feet. He froze, disgusted by the idea, and not quite sure what to do. It was bad enough to risk insulting her by refusing to eat the worm, but he knew this situation contained another menace. Recalling mythic rules from the stories he knew as a child, there was a faint remembrance that mortals must not eat or drink when they cross the veil to the Otherworld, or they would have to remain forever. Savoring the trap she had set, she commanded him to eat it, and when he did not, her demeanor darkened to offense.

Caoimhe stepped in then. "Sister, I don't think humans can eat worms." Aoife raised an eyebrow, requiring more. "I...I think they're more like us...than the creatures. They eat food that's... prepared. Cakes and sweets, and meats, and..." she trailed off, having bought them another moment to be toyed with while they looked for escape.

"Fine." She snapped her fingers, and a plate of delights and a goblet of wine appeared on the large stone next to him. "You can have no quarrel with the finest of food from my own table. Now, eat." It was clear that it was not a request.

Adrian summoned his courage, and with grave deference replied, "My Lady. I am greatly honored by your favor and have no wish to offend you. But I know that I must refuse, for if I eat of your food, I cannot return to my own land."

The air was pregnant with stillness, anticipating a lightning flash of anger. But what happened felt more like the low growl of thunder, deep and ominous. The pretense of Aoife's game dissolved, and she condescended to her little sister.

"How naive you are, Little One, to fall for the clever words of this insignificant knave." She turned a quiet fury towards Adrian. "How dare you come into our world, intending to make a prize of whichever beauty you stumbled upon first? As if you were worthy of even dreaming of such a thing."

Hot anger flared inside of Adrian—anger that she would try to taint something so beautiful, in a way that was not at all what it was like. He never intended any of this, but if she was right about anything, it was that he would not dream of being worthy of someone like Caoimhe. Except that, because of the way he felt when he was around her, somehow he did feel worthy. She made him feel that way. She made him feel in love. Fiercely, unapologetically, wholeheartedly.

Seeing the emotions written across his face, Aoife sensed an opportunity and turned on her sister. "Don't you see how he lusts for you? Don't think I don't see how tender you are with him." Caoimhe could not get a word in edgewise to defend him, and it would not have served her anyway. Aoife had written the story to her own conclusion and anyone who would try to turn the tide would be made to suffer. "This thing is not worthy of you. Your affections would be better, and more pleasurably, spent on Lord Tiernan."

Caoimhe winced at the crudeness of her sister's words, yet remained mindful of the peril Adrian was in. Summoning up a tone of resignation she hoped would appease her sister, the lie of the apathy she forced into it broke her own heart. "Fine, then, let's just let him go."

"I think not. In punishment for his trespass, he will remain here as a servant." Aoife paused, then added, as if she were being thoughtful, "If you are so fond of him, you may keep him."

But Aoife knew the cruelty of this bargain, and the lesson she meant to impart. She wasn't about to let Caoimhe's softness ruin either of their chances at court. Let her see how shallow this mortal's affections were when the indignity of servitude eroded his love for her. Or on the other hand, he could be ensorcelled to remain forever besotted and forget the world he came from, to always follow Caoimhe like a devoted dog. She could teach Caoimhe how to toy with him and take her pleasure discreetly, all the while remaining free to increase her standing in Lord Tiernan's affections.

Adrian himself could imagine worse fates than serving the one you love, but because of the truth of what they had shared between them, he knew that the arrangement was a mockery of their love. And he never expected that he would have to choose between the things he loved—being with her, or the life he called his own. Not that he was being given a choice; he was merely a fly in a spider's web.

While Adrian pondered his own heart, Caoimhe made the choice, and chose truth. The truth that Adrian would see his family again, would make his own life, and that their love would abide with dignity, even if they had to give each other up.

"What about a contest, instead?" Caoimhe said.

Aoife could not resist considering such a delicious opportunity. The young fool thought that maybe her pet had a chance of escape, or else she wouldn't risk it, but in games of intrigue she was overmatched, to be sure. Aoife could play along, and perhaps be rid of the mortal and break her sister to her will once and for all. And if she were honest, some part of her feared that keeping him around as a servant held some risk. Faery lore and legend always taught that magic allowed for escape from the most impossible situations for the smallest overlooked details.

The challenge had to be possible; the rules were clear as far as that was concerned. But the stakes had to be high enough to be worthwhile. Aoife ventured, "Shall he fight a snake?" That would be fun and solved the problem most deliciously.

Caoimhe committed to her role, determined to appear convincing and disinterested enough for Aoife to agree. "What about... making him cross a spider's web over a great height? I can command Lietanimh to build a web between the trees over the stream. If he crosses it successfully, he may return to his world." Setting the trap for Aoife, she added, "Else let him fall and die for his insolence."

Aoife didn't believe for a minute in this sudden flippant demeanor—Caoimhe obviously had faith in her subject, or a trick up her sleeve—but it was too good to pass up. "Very well. But you must agree to a binding spell—you will not be able to interfere."

The trap sprung, Caoimhe did her best to look stricken, as if beaten at her own game. She lowered her head and acquiesced sadly, then felt a cloud of energy form around her. It was warm and comfortable, but she knew that it would prevent her from touching Adrian or using any magic to help him.

It took some time for Lietanimh to build a web between the two trees. It would only have been out of reach of a tall person in the waking world, but here, the height was as if it were between two buildings, or a great chasm over a raging river. If Adrian was worried, it was not about the crossing, but Caoimhe and her sadness. Solemnly, and quietly, they watched as the web took shape. It seemed like an eternity now since the last time they had spoken to each other—since the last time it was only the two of them delighting in the world around them. He was growing weary and running out of time. But Caoimhe waited for her moment.

When Aoife's attention was fully occupied with the construction of the web, Caoimhe raised her bent head and gave Adrian a smile brighter than the sun—a look that told him she had chosen a challenge she believed he would master. Then she carefully returned her face to a solemn, distant look. He knew then that he could do anything she believed he could.

The moment arrived. Edging out onto the web, testing its springiness, he got a feel for the tension and the give of the thread. Good. He worked his way along the long single thread, focusing on the longest tightrope of his life. He became aware that the ground was so far away that if he fell, he would fall for so long before he died that the height ceased to matter. What was the difference, the height from the ground, or the length of the rope? He could do this for hours on a slackline one foot off of the ground, so he must do this the same way. There was no difference.

Both faeries hovered out of reach, following his progress from a distance. He put Aoife out of his mind. But Caoimhe he knew was there without looking. Her belief in him filled him with confidence, and he wanted her to see every step, as though he danced for her. He no longer had any doubt that he could do it, and simply was entirely present in actually doing it. It was no sorcery, just pure flow, as he made his way gradually along the line.

As he moved his way across the chasm, he reached the end of the thread anchoring the complex creation to the tree, and encountered the first radial threads which wound around the spokes, creating the web. He could see that they looked different. Raising a foot to test them, he happened to look up and see a hungry look in Aoife's face. Pulling his foot back gracefully just in time, he realized that these were the sticky threads that entangle prey. He mustn't touch them. Instead, he carefully stepped over them each time they crossed the non-sticky line.

As the distance between the threads grew too close, he had to step to other spoke lines to make his way in a semi-circle around the center. It was now the most challenge walk of his life, and he pushed what must have been Aoife's fury out of his mind, and instead, felt Caoimhe's sigh of relief flood through his body. He didn't even look, and he didn't know how, but he felt it and it gave him the strength to keep going.

But Aoife did not like to be disappointed. Keenly aware that she could not interfere with the challenge through any magic or action of her own, she wracked her mind trying to come up with some way to tip the balance in her favor. Then, she spied a fly buzzing in the air. Caoimhe was focused on the human, so she casually drifted towards the fly, making no sudden moves. When she was in range, she swatted it out of her way—no one could blame her for waving off the pesky creature after all?— and it flew immediately into the web, where it stuck fast and struggled. Lietanimh, while a devoted and good creature, could not resist instinct. As soon as the first vibration hit her, crouched on the furthest part of the web, she moved with lightning speed towards the fly, sending spasms of vibration up every thread. "Lietanimh!" Caoimhe shouted, but the spider could not contain her excitement. As Adrian bobbed on the line like a ship on a wave, the great spider reached the fly and began to wrap it, her tempo making the web sing like an instrument.

Adrian felt the sound reverberate through his body, buzzing his insides, electric. Adrenaline rushed through him, and instead of fighting it, he gently bounced the line, finding a rhythm through which he could move. He built energy when the line bowed down, and released it when he came up, sliding himself forward a little faster than he could just walking. It was time to finish this. Each bounce brought him closer to the tree, and with the last of his strength, he made the last step to solid footing. In that moment, he discovered that everything had finally come together. All of the hard work, discipline, drive, joy, centering, had needed one final ingredient to give it meaning: love. He looked up and saw Caoimhe flying towards him with joy in her face, and he reached out to embrace her.

"Well, I suppose neither of us wins, then, Sister." And with a swirl of Aoife's arm, a circle opened under him and he fell hard onto the forest floor, into the bright sunlight, surrounded by a fairy ring of mushrooms.

A Year Later

The act begins. Adrian sits contemplatively on a platform high above the crowd as the spotlight shines on him, then diffuses into a multiplicity of gentle pinks, purples, and yellows that illuminate the top of the tent—only for a moment, as they fade and another spotlight across the way draws attention to an aerialist floating down from the ceiling on wires, resplendent in gauzy wisps, shining ribbons, and larger-than-life wings that trail longer than her body. She gracefully flips and dances in the air like a ballet dancer, whose movements in turn are intended to evoke woodland sylphs. Adrian and the aerialist, Ilona, lock into a zone of pure flow; they slightly overplay their gesturing and longing faces, fueled by the excitement of performing this for the first time in front of an audience, but it only makes the scene more potent.

As the excitement builds, he can no longer contain his longing, and edges out onto the tightrope, attempting to close the gap between them. The audience applauds as he reaches the other side, but The Fairy playfully flies just out of his reach. Once again, he edges his feet over the abyss. In the middle of the scene, she flies around him laughing, and he wows the crowd by reaching for her and turning around on the wire. The audience laughs sympathetically as he jumps up and down to try to catch her, futilely. Then he sits on the wire, one leg hanging down petulantly while the other rests bent, a place to put his elbow so his head can rest sulkily on his fist. The fairy relents and comes to kiss him on the head, and, hope restored, he springs to his feet and pursues her towards the platform. The audience adores it.

This time, all seems the same, but as he chases his fairy across the rope once more, another aerialist flies in, a Bad Fairy dressed in dark purples and blacks. To him, this outfit is more inspired more by Caoimhe and her dress of butterfly wings and spider silk, while Ilona's Good Fairy resembles the splendid, overdone finery of Aoife's, but he never expected to be able to show what it was really like in the Fae. The subtle joys of that afternoon could never really be told, or even shown, but only felt. It frustrated him at first as he wrote the act, and then he realized he would have to tell the truth in a way people could feel it too. It freed him to use the visual language of color and movement to express ideas in a way that all people would understand. Somehow, he knew Caoimhe would understand the truth he was sharing.

Svetlana, as the Bad Fairy, flies in mid wire, blocking the way between them and blasts him with glittery confetti as a klieg light flares him. He doesn't even have to act as he crunches his eyes closed against the blinding light that burns through his eyelids, and falls away from its heat as the audience gasps, into a net below that, until now, the audience would not have seen was shaped like a spiderweb, as the lights had kept all attention above. But now the effect was magical, as he bounces and the web mechanically tips him out to give the audience a better view. It's a beautiful construction, cunningly woven and coated with a flexible shiny polymer paint that glitters in the light, with a few wisps of light floaty thread that catch in the current of breath and heat.

Determined, he scrambles back up the ladder, and to protect himself from her magic, dons a blindfold to make the crossing, while unseen to him, the Good Fairy floats nearby. At one moment he pauses, gently reaching, and she flutters back just a foot away.

He completes the transit to thunderous applause, acknowledging the audience for a moment.

The Bad Fairy and her sister float neutrally in the background, watching with interest. We wonder, is the Good Fairy rooting for him or merely waiting to see if he is worthy? He moves out over the line once more. We have not seen until now that a thin line between two unseen points of rigging has been suspended from the ceiling, perpendicular to the tightrope and on an angle, one end higher than the other. It is not significant looking, but we wonder why it's there.

She twirls and glitters on the other side, floating weightlessly, beautiful and ethereal.

Suddenly, a huge fantastical spider slides down the line towards him, gaining speed as it descends. It is as big as a bumper car, with a clever mechanism inside that rolls down the wire turning wheels that make the legs move. It has red glowing LED eyes, and it is beautifully horrible. The moment arrives, and with perfect timing, Adrian bounces the wire, flips in the air as it passes, and lands on the undulating tightrope. Taking the last few steps lightly, he gains the platform to thunderous applause.

The Nasty Fairy flies away, defeated, but the Good Fairy seems torn. She goes to leave, then flies in close, within reach, but he does not grab. Instead he closes his eyes for a kiss, but she flies away. But then, just like the spider, a huge sparrow slides along the rigging. Underneath its foot is a heavy-duty aerialist hand strap. He flies off the platform grabbing the "foot", and sails off into the darkness of the ceiling as the lights dim, in pursuit of his love.

The audience explodes, utterly delighted by what they've seen, and the show moves on to the next act. Backstage, Adrian accepts a few good will pats and expressions of encouragement, and then everyone dissipates for their own entrances or costume changes. Having finally found something personal and meaningful to say, he knows that now, this is really where he belongs. Alone now, he quietly closes his eyes and thinks of her. "Thank you," he whispers. Every time he performs the act, he'll think of her and remember their time together, and that she cared enough to save him.

After the show, a small, brown-haired young woman eases her way through the crowd. She's quite petite, and except perhaps for her size, unremarkable—almost invisible. Still, she has a pretty smile, and Adrian always makes time for the fans. They exchange a few pleasantries and take a picture together.

"I really liked the spider," she says. "It was funny."

"Really? It was supposed to be pretty scary," he laughs, not offended.

"No, I like little animals and things like that. Maybe it's because I grew up playing in the woods all the time."

"Me too!" He replies with excitement.

The crowd flows past them as they chat about little things they have in common, the beginnings of a web connecting little threads to each other.

Soon, it is time to go. She tells him it was nice to meet him, and they both linger for just a moment when he invites her to text him, if she wants to.

To his relief, she smiles, takes out her phone to save his number. He does not see how she gracefully wipes away a bit of cobweb that was stuck to the screen, and does not hear the quickening of her heartbeat.

Come One! Come All!

Pamela Love

Pamela Love was born in New Jersey. After graduating from Bucknell University, she worked as a teacher and in marketing before switching to writing full time. Her fiction has appeared in Cricket, Havok, Page & Spine, and Spaceports & Spidersilk, among other magazines. She lives in Maryland.

I wasn't a clown, but I got my share of laughs on my first day with the circus. Snickers, really. Millicent Dalrymple—one of those Dalrymples, which means something around here—helping to put up posters advertising elephant acts and tightrope walkers? The idea! My grandmothers were no doubt turning in their graves, but my creditors didn't care that I should be thinking about my debut, not my debts.

Some bad decisions on my father's part (I'll spare you the details) led to him skipping town ahead of those creditors—and without yours truly. Mother died years ago, so I had to support myself, which wasn't easy in the Great Depression. If I did a good job with their posters, O'Hanrahan's Circus might hire me on to sell popcorn and pop during the shows. ("You haven't the looks to be a showgirl, nor an act to join our show," Mrs. O'Hanrahan had told me when I'd come looking for work. What I did have was the height to help put up posters, and the sense not to whine when I wasn't offered something better.)

If I wasn't lucky, bad weather might cancel a show or two. Men and elephants had put up a tent the day before (and wasn't that a sight to see), so rain wouldn't be a problem. But, a strong enough wind could knock that same tent down. Mrs. O'Hanrahan wouldn't want that kind of trouble.

If I was really unlucky, a downpour might peel off the posters I'd put up—and if all three dozen weren't up until the circus left town, I wouldn't be paid.

So, I crossed my toes (my fingers being otherwise occupied) as I glanced up at the thunderheads moving in. I definitely wasn't thinking about how I was standing on a ladder as I finished smoothing out a poster, at least not until my hair started standing on end. By then it was too late to do anything but say a word that must've accelerated my grandmothers' grave spinning. Out of the corner of my eye, I saw Billy leap to safety. An acrobat couldn't have done better than that roustabout.

I woke up staring at the sky and Billy's face. "You okay?"

I wiggled my toes—still crossed. Maybe that was what kept me from dying when the lightning struck. Not being dead, I still had a job to do. "Let's go." While Billy grabbed the ladder, I looked around for the paste bucket. It turned out to be lying on its side, spilling its goo down the gutter. I must've knocked it over when I fell.

What I said then no doubt made my grandmothers give up on me altogether. What I did then...I still can't explain the how or why of it, unless it was the crossed toes.

Billy echoed what I'd just said, but not about the missing paste. No, he was wrestling with the posters. There wasn't any wind, but it was like they were a bunch of flags, all flapping in their own little twister.

One of them peeled off and stuck itself on my hands—the picture side, that is. That was all I needed, to tear it. My fingers twitched—and the poster hovered in front of them.

I don't mind telling you, it was eerie. I jumped back a foot, and the poster leaped against the wall—and stayed there.

Billy's jaw dropped a foot. He took a step back. "Don't hurt me, witch."

I rolled my eyes. "Don't be silly. It's just static. Haven't you ever seen static hold something on your sweater?"

Billy had worked around elephants the day before, but I guess I was scarier because he took off down the street. That meant I still had to get dozens of posters up, which was really a job for two.

As it turned out, the static was still with me. I was able to put up every last poster for O'Hanrahan's Circus all by myself, without any paste at all. And wasn't that a sight to see?

I did some experimenting overnight and some hard thinking as well. I still wanted to join the circus all right—but my dreams had changed.

Polly O'Hanrahan was a busy lady. She'd already made up her mind about me, and I doubted she'd give me a second look. Actions speak louder than words, so I'd just have to show that my actions could draw a crowd.

At first, they were too busy to notice me that morning. So, I finally bawled out (in tones that Miss Elton of Miss Elton's Charm School would never have approved of), "ladies and gentlemen!"

That got some attention since it's not every day that the Big Top has a girl crawling up the side of it. Attention and applause, and that meant something to me since I'd never had much of a talent for anything.

As far as I knew, I was one of a kind. That meant money—an act, a career! Oh, I'd need a costume, but Polly O'Hanrahan would take care of that. Or maybe I should join a bigger show, which could pay more.

Someone hollered at me through a megaphone to come on down, and I did just that. I could see myself a big star, all right. Come one, come all! See the Marvelous Millicent!

What I couldn't see were the flames starting to lick at my heels, but the roustabouts certainly did. If the clowns hadn't had a "funny firemen" act, complete with a pump full of water, that fire would've gotten out of control in a hurry. As it turned out, I left a hole about six feet wide, which meant taking down the whole Big Top, patching it in a hurry, and setting it back up again before the afternoon's show. That may have been more of a miracle than my lightning bolt.

Mrs. O'Hanrahan was far kinder about everything than I deserved. She took the time to sit down with me once everything was organized. "Your act is wonderful, but it's too dangerous. Circus tents are covered with wax. The grandstands are made of wood, and sawdust covers the floors. Circus folk—and our animals—fear fire more than anything else. And, I can't risk taking you on as a butcher—that's what we call our food vendors—in case your static strikes another spark. Do you understand?" I nodded, not trusting myself to speak. I wanted to tell her I'd pay her back for what I'd done, but it's not as if I had many employment opportunities.

She bit her lip. "Billy told me about the lightning. I'm sorry about that. Sometimes strange things happen around circuses. I've seen a dozen things I can't explain."

"So I'm unlucky thirteen."

"There's magic out there, Millicent Dalrymple, and circus folk sometimes call some of it down to us. That lightning could've killed you. It didn't. Maybe you don't know why yet, but I'd bet my tent you'll find out someday."

I walked away slowly, but I didn't stop going until the sun went down. Truthfully, I kept on going even when I couldn't see, into the woods surrounding my home town. By that point, I wasn't sure I cared where I was going.

I certainly didn't care enough to dodge very hard when lightning started striking nearby. I half-wondered if my "magic" or whatever it was would go away if another bolt struck me. Just in case, I crossed my toes. You never know.

Worn out, I sat back against a tree to rest. I watched the lightning, and resented it, and wrapped my mind around it, I suppose. It took some doing, but I remembered that lightning was a kind of electricity, just like static. And, I could make it do what I wished with plenty of practice. High overhead, of course. I'd learned my lesson.

I knew where O'Hanrahan's Circus was going. I'd seen their schedule. And so did the rest of the state, thanks to the letters I wrote across the sky in lightning, every night for a month. Come one! Come all! See O'Hanrahan's Circus, The Most Wonderful Show of All!

With some research at the library, I found a new name for my profession. "Marvelous Millicent" wasn't appropriate for my advertising business. What I finally settled on would've been better for a circus act, but by then every circus in the world wanted my help, so I guess it really does suit me.

After all, what's a circus without an ion tamer?

Skyboss

Rocky Breen

Rocky Breen grew up in a mobile home on a homestead farm in Michigan. She fenced for four years and practiced jujitsu for three. Her hobbies now include trail running, gardening, knitting, letter-writing, and cooking. Rocky is American, earned a B.A. in Linguistics, and has second language proficiency in Japanese. Currently, her writing projects include a fantastical romance, some fanfiction, and a couple of audio dramas.

On May 28, 2056, the Strato Circus would dazzle the world with a special show highlighting the approach of the blue-hued Comet Stephan–Oterma. And at CBB News, one reporter needed to go up to cover it. Camille was determined it be her.

When she was in the third grade, her parents bought her a glossy astronomy book. She was the only Black kid in her grade at Love Elementary, but she was *not* the only kid interested in the stars, so after Xiomara—*supposed* friend—almost ripped one of the pages, Camille took to reading it only over breakfast at home. With her dad grumbling about Pluto (*"Dwarf planet,* my ass. Ya' book is *wrong"*), every morning that spring she flipped through the pages as he served breakfast. Devouring whatever he made with a grin, her heart would beat fast as she looked at photos of the planets, photos of earth from the star-studded black of space, reading how small humans really were in the grand scheme of things. Camille wondered at charts of planetary mass (Jupiter was 1300 Earths' big!) and marveled at human ingenuity to the point of putting drones on Mars and sending satellite explorers out into the Oort Cloud.

Even now, Camille had her telescope manual memorized, and emails regularly peppered her inbox to remind her of upcoming astronomical appearances.

She didn't grow up to be an astronaut, and the Strato Circus wasn't technically an opportunity to go to space. But at thirty-seven years old, she knew this was the closest she'd ever get. From a visual perspective it was still a perfect emulation, even if she wouldn't be weightless up there.

So Camille fought hard for and won the assignment. Even so, it was a battle to get hazard pay upfront. "What if I die up there?" she asked her supervisor pointedly. She knew for a fact that James McLennon, the white journalist who'd covered the rocky debut of the Strato Circus five years prior and nearly died along with the whole circus crew as he did so, had fought hard for front-loaded hazard pay...and won.

Her supervisor took it up the chain when she cited that fact. The hazard pay was deposited in her bank account three days later. While most of it would go into savings, she considered using some of the money to buy a full 81-key Smart keyboard for her daughter's birthday instead of the smaller 69-key one that was wrapped up in the closet.

"Half of the time, their interest fizzles out after they get a gift like this—guitar, snowboard, whatever—it's hard work to get good, and if we don't get her a coach, she won't continue after the initial shine wears off," her wife, Li, argued. She'd gotten Shuri a new VR game with that exact logic. "Besides, she's only seven. An 81-key monster might be discouraging since Shuri's arms don't even go out that wide."

"Says the woman who was playing concertos at that age."

Li had sighed and said, "I love my mother, but I hate the piano now and it's hard enough to even *let* Shuri have one. It's not like I ever became a professional pianist, anyway."

They'd named Shuri after Camille's favorite superhero growing up, with an additional nod to a classical novelist Li enjoyed, Zhao Shuli. Plus, Camille secretly hoped that her daughter would follow the mathematical, science route that she herself hadn't pursued. At the moment, it seemed like Shuri would defy both her parents by loving music best.

Three weeks before the event, a Circus athlete was injured, which postponed the date. The new date meant Camille was going to miss Shuri's eighth birthday.

Li side-eyed her something fierce when this came up, and Shuri cried because she was worried about Mama going up at all, but Camille wanted this assignment and wasn't going to miss out. This was her chance. She smiled just thinking of the view. Sometimes she still kicked herself for not pursuing physics. Though the math might have gotten her to NASA and to being an astronaut, journalism was taking her close enough.

Besides, Camille was tired of covering the election cycle. Let someone else talk about poll numbers for a minute. Mama was going to see space.

In preparation, Camille watched the historic Red Bull Stratos jump. An outspoken neo-Nazi Austrian daredevil floated up in a weather balloon back in 2018. That man jumped thirty-seven years before the days of her research, but the video quality was good enough to make her nauseous as she watched his leap from the open bottom of the metal balloon basket.

And yet, compared to that nauseating clip, her actual assignment would be much more dangerous. Not as dangerous as a warzone, perhaps, but dangerous enough that she'd be wearing a protective suit of her own, equipped with a parachute—just in case—and given a 'crash course' (they thought they were hilarious, but the pun only pissed her off) in knowing how to skydive in case the balloon failed to descend properly.

Additionally, this year, the azure-haloed Stephan-Oterma Comet in the background of the Circus would add another layer of spectacle...and danger. Camille reached out to multiple sources for comment, and one astronomer, Dr. Bannerjee at MIT, warned, "Normally comets keep their distance, but ah, no, not this one. Whatever respect the Circus usually pays to atmospheric conditions needs to triple. Comets come with their own gravity, their own magnetosphere, their own dust and debris, and the atmosphere levels above the Circus offer incomplete protection to its athletes."

With two weeks before lift-off, The Ringleader, a white man in his forties with an athletic build, a handlebar mustache, and a failed tan that aged him prematurely said, "The show must go on. And the Circus, why, it's all about skirtin' danger, ain't it? Always has been. We'll do as much prep'ration as we can on the day of to make sure our staff and facility can safely lift off, 'n we will continue to take precautions as we fly 'n as we descend. But at the ind of the day, there will always be some randim eliments that we cannot account for. I've asked! But we cannot predict how, when, or where this comet may affect us."

That was a broadcast interview, and it made Camille squirm internally; she'd been raised in Texas, and while it had *plenty* of idiots, there were also plenty of good and intelligent folks, regardless of education level, and she squirmed because his response reinforced that 'reckless Southerner' stereotype.

Camille was familiar enough with comets at this point in her research and personal hobby that she believed the astronomer over the Ringleader. But it intrigued her that the acrobats put their faith in the Ringleader anyway.

Finally, Camille researched the history of circuses, looking for tidbits she could slip into her reporting to establish context for audiences or hook them with intrigue. Naturally, Romans and colonialist Europeans showed up first in her search. She skipped Sarah Baartman and other so-called 'freak shows'—too painful to read about, and also not TV-friendly for reporting on the Strato Circus, whose only freaks were the acrobats bold enough to participate. Phillip Astley and Jane Jones' equestrian tricks in the 1770s looked quaint next to the Strato Circus, where the athletes jumped and danced with mecha-enhanced suits from one platform to another, the fall a distance of 38,000 meters instead of just one.

On the morning of lift-off, the quiet buzz of activity vibrated in her bones. She readied herself in front of her small news crew. It wasn't lost on her that she was the only Black person onsite with CBB, the shade of her warm-brown skin neared only by Ria's coppery tones. Everybody else was white or passed for it.

Spring mornings in the desert were *cold*. Camille's wool blazer and white-collared shirt didn't keep all the chill away from her skin. The microphone in her hand was frigid. She stepped back and checked her looks in the camera van's window. Her "warrior" goddess braids (Shuri's term) shone with silver cuffs matching Shuri's for the occasion ("Like *stars*," her little girl had said reverently). She stepped forward in place again, testing the mic. The soundman nodded. Ria, her camera-lady, gave her the thumbs up.

Then, in her earpiece, she heard the anchor in the newsroom introduce her. "As promised, Camille Luo-Jones is at the Roswell International Air Centre in New Mexico, our bravest correspondent. I'd take a thousand war zones over flying up to space like you, Camille."

She laughed for the red dot of the camera and code-switched to her news reporter voice. "You're too kind, James. And while I'm certainly here for the view of space, the name says it all: Strato Circus. The stratosphere isn't technically space, but it *is* above the Armstrong Limit, where water boils at body temperature. It doesn't get more space-like than that for non-astronauts. And this year, we'll have the view of a comet to top it all at the big top.

"Preparing for ascent behind me, you can see dozens of weather balloons being inflated by those cherry-picker-looking machines. They'll all float up together tethered around that white, netted drone kite that the Circus calls 'the big top.' Up there, it will serve as their stage and also a way of keeping the balloons from knocking into each other.

"Thirty minutes from now, twenty-four acrobats, five circus managers, ten spectators, and five reporters like myself will board and begin checks for lift-off. They'll check cameras, radios, and most importantly, the air and pressure-management and life-sustaining systems on board."

"Camille, since you're one of the reporters going up, what have they told you to expect?"

"Well, like the acrobats, I'll be wearing a full-pressure suit, hooked up to umbilical air supply for ascent..."

Camille went on just as she'd practiced with her notecards, eyes firmly on camera, smiling every few seconds, determinedly not looking over at her wife or their little birthday girl touring the premises.

"And what are you looking forward to most?" Now Camille was interviewing Timothy Grandrix, arrogant British billionaire she not-so-secretly hated.

More than circuses of the past, the Strato Circus audience could get in on the danger. Wealthy spectators went up solo in their own re-fitted weather balloons billed 'skyboxes.' Tickets went for millions, and every returnee got a commemorative pin in the shape of a rocket-like hot-air balloon.

Timothy Grandrix went every year, and every year on TV, he purposefully mispronounced "Skybox" as "Skyboss," just as he did now with a grin. His pink fingers tapped the last five years' pins on his lapel and said, "This'll be my 6th *Skyboss* year, and I've never been more excited. No light pollution to fight with to see the comet up there."

If it weren't for him, Camille would actually have been more excited to receive her own pin. A bubble of envy and determination floated up in her belly, looking at his six pins. Well, she'd have one, and that was more than most people in the world could say. And hers would be a special year, with not just the weather balloon insignia but also the emblem of a comet flying over in blue and red.

"We've got to move on, but we'll check back with you when you and the acrobats start loading up for the stratosphere! Thanks, Camille."

"Can't wait, James."

The truth was, now her nerves were getting to her. She handed the mic off to the recording crew, put on her coat, and walked the desert gravel towards her family, trying to distract herself by simply observing the things around her. Underfoot, sand and stone crunched beneath her boots. The sky was dawn cerulean turning paler and paler. In front of a blood-red weather balloon, she saw Timothy Grandrix laughing with Nikhi Patel, a tech magnate with only a slightly better personality than Grandrix. North of them, the famous Macedonian acrobat Mihaela Janevski stood with her solar-themed team, gleaming in their golden suits and posing for photos with the small crowd of fans.

When she found Shuri and Li, Shuri was bouncing up and down, waving her arms in front of one of the mecha animal kites that had lifted up and buoyed at the end of its tether in the air. It looked like a crane, and she heard Shuri asking Mommy to remind her the Chinese word for it. Camille watched them for a moment. Camille had her secrets, but she was a performer, never shy. Those two, though, had in common that they blossomed in the wild, away from crowds.

Camille walked up to her daughter, whose skin was just a shade lighter than hers and glowed in the sunlight. She crouched down. "Hi, Shuri," she said gently. Shuri turned, beamed, and before she could lean in for a hug, Camille wiped crumbs from her daughter's mouth, laughing. "Mug cake," she said, and Shuri laughed adorably. Before leaving the house, they had made a spontaneous dessert because breakfast hadn't quite hit the spot.

Camille squeezed her daughter tight and grinned up over her gemmed braids at Li, who smiled down softly. When Camille stood up again, Li surprised her with a brush of her fingers across her cheek. Li wasn't big on PDA.

Camille grinned and pushed that envelope. "No cameras, Li-li. Don't I get a kiss before my life-threatening trip to space? If you say no, you and Shuri better be comin' up there with me."

Li rolled her eyes, mumbling, "You're so embarrassing." Her cool beige skin faded to dark bags beneath her eyes. She wasn't the type to say she was worried or beg Camille not to go. But she must have been worried anyway. She scanned for onlookers.

Seemingly convinced she wouldn't really be embarrassed, Li pulled Camille's face closer and kissed her sweetly.

Camille's nerves came back. Sweet as that kiss was, it just reminded her that if the right things went wrong up in stratos, it could be her last. She pulled back a bit and rubbed her nose against Li's. Li smiled, then frowned.

"Be safe up there and come back to us, ok?"

"Mama, Mommy, can I go, too? Please?"

It was about the eight hundredth time her baby girl had asked. "Maybe next time, Shuri."

Camille smiled and checked at her watch just as Ria hollered her name. "Camille! It's time!"

She gave them each one last hug and tried not to cry.

Inside a tent, she changed into a special wet-suit-looking garment, then into the heavy full-pressure suit itself. The cameras were on her— "a more relatable view than the acrobats" was the strangest sort of compliment James had ever tried to pay her, but she decided to take it as one. This was her job, in a way. Showing newsworthy events. She let herself be a little more clumsy than she liked on-screen. Giggled a little more than strictly necessary. It was an act, but it helped with her nerves.

"This thing is *heavy*. If you've ever been pregnant, or worn those weight suits to simulate it, think about twice as heavy. Thank goodness I'm not one of the acrobats. All I have to do is sit in a bucket floating up there. They must be benching and squatting a *lot* to get to this strength and do jumps and dances up there."

"Having second thoughts?" James asked in her earpiece.

"Not a chance," Camille said.

Last of all came the helmet. Good thing she wasn't claustrophobic, as this would have been the coffin lid closing.

A big, reflective number twenty-one was painted on her weather balloon. She stepped inside and sat down as they instructed.

They buckled her in to the air and fluid-supply systems and showed her the different controls she needed to know. Hatch release, untethering, monitors, comms, camera angling, heat, air, outside mirrors, lights. Then they closed the door with only Camille inside.

James and other anchors kept engaging her with chitchat every few minutes while she waited. Her fishbowl-like window, which was two times as wide and tall as her face, showed her a smaller view of the outside than she wanted. She did have a monitor, which would let her see and comment on the acrobatics once they were in stratos.

Outside, the Circus tech in front of the CBB camera crew faced her and counted down with their hands from 10, and Camille vocalized it for the camera and mic on her chest looking out.

"Three, two, one, lift-off!"

This time, her giggle was real glee. Her stomach dropped as her balloon began ascending. It was like being on a Ferris wheel, only this one just kept climbing up and up, stopping once not far off the ground to be tethered to the kite drone, then up and up again.

The ascent was singular, but only because of what she knew was occurring, the height she was climbing from her seat in this little capsule. Alone. That was frightening. But otherwise, the two and a half-hour climb proceeded like a slow airplane flight.

She stopped looking out the window in glee, scanning the clear blue sky and the desert landscape below. Initial excitement led to boredom, and she cued up a podcast in between check-in times with the news crew. She started to get cold, then between the suit and the weather balloon, she was warm again. Her first pee in the space-diaper (her word for it) felt embarrassing and gross, but the second one felt much more matter-of-fact.

The view shifted gradually, but finally, she got what she came for. At just over 37,000 meters up, she looked out the fishbowl window. She stared at the curve of the blue earth against the black mouth of space. The sun was behind her and to the right, lighting up the west coast below and chasing the dark from the Pacific. The comet was nowhere to be seen yet, but she expected that. They told her it would likely be out of sight from her window for a bit, but the cameras would catch it.

Clouds nearby cast long shadows, while clouds far away dazzled in the light. They rotated and expanded gently like pinwheels remembering a long-ago summer breeze. Deep, inky blackness as far as the eye could see. The moon not any bigger or closer, half-gleaming in the far distance. She felt at peace. She felt like she could stay here forever.

She struggled to remember the lines of an Anne Spencer poem, "Earth, I thank you," but the words didn't come, only the sense that the feeling from that poem was so similar to what she felt now, the title so apt for this experience.

But work called. Camille blinked a few times and sighed as her earpiece played music. The Strato Circus was starting, the old Blazes and Thunder theme revamped with electronic inspiration. They didn't play the music out here, relying instead on everyone's helmet speakers for timing, though they did their best at lighting and recording. The AV crew on earth added the sound, and that's what she was hearing.

It all felt like crashing chaos, an insult to the quiet moment of awe she'd just experienced.

"You're up," Ria from CBB told her. On the monitor, she saw James in the newsroom. His brown beard was gone, and Camille thought he looked like one of those cherubs from the Sistine Chapel. She pushed a button on her helmet to make the face shield clear instead of tinted with the camera facing her.

"Our very own Camille has a front-row seat to the Strato Circus," James said. "Camille, how was the ascent?"

She composed herself as best she could sitting in her own pee. "It was uneventful, which is a blessing for an operation as delicate as this one. The real danger, though, begins now..."

Camille repeated the same highlights as before. This part of broadcast reporting annoyed her. You had to assume you were catching an audience member entirely new to the subject, and the repetition bored her.

She signed off after and watched the monitor.

A pre-recorded clip of Ringleader and performers down on earth introduced the event. "Welcome to Strato Circus 6, 2056!"

Camille leaned back to see the monitor, which flicked to and from the different weather balloons tethered together around the drone kite like spoke ends on a wheel. "This is a special year, with the Stephan-Oterma Comet lighting up the night sky. Even without a telescope, you can see it!"

Camille laughed to herself, hearing that. Plenty of those places with clouds wouldn't see anything. But then, across the monitor, a lightly jostling view of the blue-white comet over one of their weather balloons chilled her to the bone. It really was stunning. But it was also *really* big and close. Bigger than the moon. She remembered historical illustrations of comets, folks fearing their lives were about to end, the world going down with them. She understood why.

The Ringleader went on and on, but Camille was trying to remember her emergency instructions, looking for the handle that (*heart attack*) she could pull to open the hatch of her weather balloon to descend to earth.

If the comet was that big, that visible, its magnetosphere was many more times that and could easily interfere with their communications and with the atmospheric conditions they were relying on.

She was a *fool* coming up here.

Eyes closed, ignoring the debut information of one of the Strato Circus performers, she remembered something from that book— the book her parents got her, which was on display in a place of honor on her bookshelf at home. The section about comets described a flyby near Mars forty-some years back. Earth had just sent a satellite out that way and it was clear that the comet's coma stretched a million kilometers in every direction. The comet fly-by literally blew away part of Mars' upper atmosphere and messed with the planet's own magnetosphere.

Mars is different, she told herself. *Thinner atmosphere. No reason to panic.*

She confirmed that her weather balloon's cameras were responding to cues from Earth as the first acrobat stepped up. Xinyue Wang, decked in silver like the other moon acrobats, appeared in sight of the monitors. This was the new recruit. They made it out like it was a hazing ritual to send her out first alone, but actually, it was safer that way. No one to bump into, or be bumped by, right before your 38000-foot drop to Earth. On the monitors and flashing in her fishbowl window, one of the mecha animal kites prepared to join Xinyue, this one shaped like a hare, chrome hind legs gracefully bounding as Xinyue's weather balloon opened.

Camille held her breath, watching. The music in her ears stopped. Xinyue leaned out and plummeted. It was like she vanished.

Camille looked to the monitors and breathed again as the percussion alone drummed up and led into violins while the mecha kite hare's cameras and Xinyue's bodycams watched each other descending to earth.

Ria cued Camille up to give a word about this.

"Absolutely breathtaking," Camille reported truthfully. "To watch this kind of bravery first-hand, it's terrifying and exhilarating. Xinyue will descend another three minutes or so before engaging her parachute, where she'll have a controlled descent for another three or four minutes. She had a beautiful jump, no spinning—for those used to ground circuses you might think that's poor performance, but spins can be fatal in skydiving from here. That kind of smooth jump is difficult to arrange from up this high."

Music in her ears indicated she had to wrap up, so she did, and the Ringleader's pre-recorded voice again introduced the next acrobats.

"Mario Deido and Taiwo Solarin, the sun brothers—watch them step out onto the big top and bound off the edge of the world!"

Camille felt sick with worry. She shouldn't. She knew how this went. But still, her stomach clenched as she watched. Weather balloon doors in the east and west swung outward, and the red and gold-suited 'brothers' leaped forward. As they landed on the big top, the whole kite drone rocked, her weather balloon jostled, and she screeched, clasping the handrails in her capsule.

On her monitors, she watched the sun brothers grasp at the net on the top of the drone kite and climb across its surface towards each other in synchrony. All the weather balloons around the big top jiggled as they did.

"*I'm gonna die,*" she said to herself. It was as much a statement of how she felt as of what she *feared.*

The light show began when they reached the center and paused. Her balloon stabilized like a boat in a gentle current. Red and orange flame-shaped light projected onto the kite, the light shifting, fanning out from their bodies like a classical sun illustration. Mario and Taiwo's bodies mirrored each other in stiff dance moves, like two halves of a sun as the lights flashed around them. Then they moved on, each to the opposite direction. They must have had some beat-keeping measure in their earpieces to keep them grasping the net at the same time, opposite places, to keep the bouncing of the big top to a minimum.

Two more mecha kites, one dragon in crimson, the other in gold, unfurled from their tethers and descended first, letting out plumes of gold and red gas behind them. The brothers each stood at the ends of the big top and in Camille's ear, the music stopped again. The brothers leaned out and plummeted.

Chasing their dragons, they did spin. Mario, in red, even flipped, and Camille gasped. She didn't think it was on purpose. She remembered the Romans, the creators of the original circus, the original way to feel sick to your stomach but unable to look away at the breakneck race before your eyes.

The producers spun it well. They left Camille and the audience on a cliff's edge and jumped back to Xinyue, showing clips both of her in free fall, then launching her parachute, then finally gliding to a mecha-powered sprint on the ground. When she finally stood still, she pumped her fist in the air as her silvery-white parachute pillowed down. Then she dropped to her knees and let the EMT's and Circus techs inspect her.

The ground team whispered to Camille that she was fine, no injuries, and Camille beamed for the camera. "Xinyue Wang is the newest member of the Moon wing of the Strato Circus, and she exacted her jump with perfection. I'll never get over watching the acrobats land and do their bow or their curtsy, and then just let the adrenaline out by falling to the ground those last few inches. I can only imagine how difficult it is to stand after falling to earth for nine minutes straight."

The music changed, she signed off again, and the Ringleader began introducing the Star Twins.

But the big top started shaking again. Unlike when the brothers had been out on the kite, now, no one was out there and the rocking was consistent. Camille radioed to her team below. "Any updates I'm missing?"

The music went grainy and faded in and out like weak radio reception in the woods. She could hear Ria from the CBB news team speaking, but the signal kept cutting out, chopping words in half.

Camille tried to breathe calmly. But if she couldn't communicate with the team below or hear the production, the performers couldn't either. She remembered that they planned for this, that the Ringleader made the ultimate decision with either blinking red or blue lights on the outside of his weather balloon. Blue lights signaled the show would be canceled and they would begin a slow and controlled descent back down to earth. Red lights indicated immediate abortion of the operation, and in order, the balloon occupants would all descend to Earth by free-fall.

Minutes passed. Camille felt more and more uneasy as her balloon continued to shake and then bob in tandem with the others tethered to her. All audio stopped, nothing but static clogging her ears, so she turned the volume down. The monitors were blank. There must not have been any communication with the satellites.

She looked through her fishbowl window and watched the mecha kites remaining. A wolf. A dolphin. A crane. She wished she could see her fellow humans' faces, but the balloons opposite her were half a football field away, behind their own fishbowl windows and helmets.

The big top rotated and finally she could see the comet firsthand, not through a camera monitor. Only it didn't look the same... It looked muddled, amorphous, wider...Had it split up? She remembered reading about Shoemaker-Levy 9 breaking up into dozens of pieces and hitting Jupiter back in 1992.

Difficult as it was to take her eyes off the comet, she looked over at the Ringleader's weather balloon, painted with a shining number one, but no lights signaled, yet.

"-you read?"

Audio crackled in her ear and she turned it up. "I read. This is Camille of CBB News, over."

"Jump-jump-jump—copy? You-....-time. Jump. Roswell out."

"What? I have to jump? We're supposed to go in order-"

"-s no time. Jump. Over"

Heart. Attack. She was going to die of a heart attack before she died of anything else. She looked up at the comet, almost out of view as her balloon rocked more and more and twisted. Camille wondered what the matter was exactly, the journalist in her seeking answers. She wondered if she should listen to the person cutting in and out.

"Who is this?"

That was a stupid question. Her eyes went wide as she watched weather balloons opposite her swing open, occupants of numbers eighteen and twenty, both acrobats in metallic suits, jump one after the other. They must have heard the announcement, too. Now it was her turn.

Camille froze. Even as her balloon bounced and swung on its tether and she knew she needed to jump sooner rather than later, before this thing upended itself or worse—burst somehow. Camille felt tears well up in her eyes. She was alone. She was about to plummet to the earth alone or else—what? Die up here first? Why couldn't she just float down in the slow, controlled two-and-a-half-hours like she was supposed to? She'd been overreacting earlier—no way the comet was that close, and if it were, would it make that much of a difference if she were back on earth?

Yes. Yes it would, she knew. She just didn't like what that meant.

"Roswell to-...ning balloons, you need-...now. Jump now. Press the-....n to open the-"

They were reciting the instructions. She was stiff as a board, unmoving, until she thought of Shuri and Li. She began breathing deeply. She remembered that today was her baby girl's birthday. And she let out a giant exhale. Shuri's birthday would *not* be Camille's death day if she could do something about it. And according to the annoying folks at Roswell, it seemed that she could.

Camille let that annoyance take primary place in her mind as she began trying to stabilize her balloon by shifting her weight counter to its wobbles. She took one brief last glimpse at the velvet backdrop of space behind the blue-white curve of Earth. She pressed the button and hydraulics pushed the hatch open. Her stomach flipped, looking down at the earth below. All she had to do was press the button to release the drone kite tether and step out.

That's all.

It's simple, she thought. *We're making a mug cake. Just mix-*

"-have to jump-...know it's scary-"

She felt annoyed again and slammed the right button. She felt a distant scrape along the hull of her weather balloon reverb through her boots. The kite drone tether was released, her weather balloon stabilizing a bit more now that it wasn't hooked to the others, but it still swayed in an unexpected wind.

-and pop it in the microwave.

Camille leaned out, swallowed bile, and plummeted.

Or, she thought she plummeted. Strangely, it felt more like swimming without feeling water against her skin. Or like flying, for a time. She may as well have been treading water. A part of her relaxed at this. Even as wind whistled past her helmet distantly, and her mind was screaming at the reality it recognized, she also knew she had a few minutes before she needed to release the parachute, and it looked like she got her weightlessness experience after all. All simulated. She was very weighted and very much plummeting towards the earth, she knew that. But she counted her lucky stars that she was flying right, as far as she knew: belly down, hands forced up, knees bent. No spinning.

Camille wondered if the cameras back in the capsule and on her suit were running local storage or if they only streamed using satellite. Footage of this incident, at some point, would surely end up in the news cycle. Camille knew that she should try narrating for that benefit, but she was barely able to keep it together as the features of the earth became less blurry and much closer.

"Hello? Can anyone hear me?" She was greeted by static and choppy words that just made her more nervous, so she turned the speakers down again.

In descent, the suits and parachutes were automatic with manual overrides as necessary. Camille was not an expert, so she hoped she didn't have to do this manually. She cued the helmet visor to display the altitude, just in case. She waited like they told her to, feeling far calmer than she expected to at first, marveling at the landscape, but she grew more nervous as time passed. There were no clouds beneath her and the ground became visible in greater detail faster and faster.

A beeping from the speakers inside her helmet signaled that the parachute was about to deploy. When it did, it yanked her back suffocatingly, straps across her thighs and chest digging in like seat belts in a car crash. She'd be bruised. But hopefully, she'd be alive.

Her free-fall suspended, she glided towards the ground. Her

heart wasn't done pounding. The ground met her sooner than she imagined, coming up faster and faster and her abs hurt holding her legs out in front of her, toes pointed up like they told her to do. She was no acrobat. She had to land in the safest possible way for a rookie, and this was it.

Camille landed. It felt like running into a glass door as the bottoms of her thighs and butt skidded across gravel. She was thankful the suit was thick, thankful for everything that got her here alive and in one piece.

Her forward movement slowed and stopped. The yellow parachute puffed around her, gently falling.

Finally still, Camille gasped like goldfish on the counter. Her heartbeats were the wheels of a train, whirring then breaking as they came in to the station. Her hands shook wildly and her arms weren't strong enough to lift them.

Like a flash, she recalled the 'crash course' training in skydiving. They'd said that, in case of an accident, she should still descend somewhere in New Mexico.

Still chugging air, she swallowed and coughed. Her mouth was too dry. She looked around her. Desert. Sand. Cacti. A soft breeze blowing shadowy dust around. Plateaus and strange rock pillars in the distance. They must have been right.

She flopped to her back, trying to calm her breathing, but her body hadn't done anything to really work the adrenaline out, so it kept pumping through her. Looking up, she squinted against the sun and slapped the button to tint her face shield, hands still jittery and frail.

The remnants of the Strato Circus descended nearby. She saw two parachutes deploy, blue and red, the people attached small as ants. Part of her thought she should move. One of the other jumpers might land on her. But the grown-ass woman side of her was tired and felt that most likely, nothing would land on her and if they did, they did. It wasn't like she was bound to be any luckier moving fifty feet north or south. It wasn't like she could outrun anything dropping from the stratosphere, even if it were slowed down by a parachute.

So Camille laid back on the ground like she was star-gazing, hoping that the impact of her fall had scared any scorpions away, hoping that if they did come near her, this thick-ass suit would keep them off, at least.

She remembered a train trip her family had taken when she was in middle school to go to the White Sands Park in New Mexico. From Houston, it was only a three-hour bullet train ride. The sand there sparkled like snow, the world quieter than she'd ever known. But the best part for Camille had been the Perseid meteor shower, viewed from where they lay on yoga mats outside their tent.

This felt a lot like that as she closed her eyes and remembered the fantastic view she'd seen from the stratosphere.

Camille wanted a cold shower and a hot bath. She wanted cuddles and kisses and sex. She wanted to make her daughter a belated birthday breakfast and wrap up everyone she loved in the biggest bear hug. She wanted to sleep for a million years and take the longest, laziest vacation ever.

Part of her was tense and afraid to find out what it meant that the comet had come this close to Earth. Had it broken up, like Shoemaker–Levy 9? If it had, what would that mean for their already unstable climate? What would it mean days or weeks from now as they continued to orbit the sun and eventually passed through that debris?

Why had the Ringleader failed to signal? Why had Roswell Air Center told her to jump so adamantly? What was happening up there?

But all that, she decided, would come later. For now, she felt twelve years old again, opening her eyes to track the comet, its dissipation less noticeable down here, just looking like a tiny, light smudge against the bright blue sky. She watched the last of the mecha kites glide down, parachutes behind them. The crane her daughter had admired parked itself just a hundred feet away, looking silly with both wings and a parachute. Supposedly they had GPS on all these things, but the satellites had been out, so...

Her radio blared, the sounds of the rest of the world demanding her answer, demanding she report if she were alive, what was her condition, what was her location?

Camille sighed, admiring the comet for one last moment. She was exhausted, and reporting back to these people in a voice they expected of her was a more noticeable process than usual.

"CBB News correspondent Camille Luo-Jones here, seemingly alive and well. I've landed in the desert, middle of nowhere, Earth. Over."

She tried to think of a not-uncool way to get Shuri and Li to call her 'Skyboss' even just once, remembering with a smile the comet-blazing Skybox pin they had to give her now and the view of space she'd gotten to see up close.

The Mirror of Longing

Wen-yi Lee

Wen-yi Lee is a Singaporean writer currently based in London. Her works are forthcoming with Luna Station Quarterly, Strange Horizons, Speculative City and Sword & Kettle Press.

The people are bemused when they see the circus wagons wheel into town, churning up dust in their wake. There are the horses, with promises of silver hats; there are the lions, gold and lithe behind the bars; there is the strongman, twirling his mustache at the head of the caravan; there are the quintuplet acrobats, dressed in a quintuplet of plum doublets; there is the contortionist, twisted and beaming. Right at the end of the procession, where eager eyes turn to find glimpses of the circus' exotic oddities, there is only a strange, plain caravan, marked THE MIRROR OF LONGING.

That night, when the big top goes up, the townspeople flood into the seats, streaming through the box office, their coins clinking and clattering across the counter faster than the sleepy-eyed boy can tear off tickets. The show is spectacular and the applause ripples across the rest of the town, evoking envy in all those who had decided to stay home. The audience flows out chattering in wonder and seeking the nearest barkeep. But some eyes are drawn to that singular caravan parked in the shadow of the tent. Those who do slow inadvertently in their steps, drawn by some strange compulsion. Most move on.

Peter Oleander does not. His fists are stuffed in his pockets as he walks out of the show, angry steps cursing at the hot night wind. Crushed beneath his knuckles are two tickets, one untorn. Estelle Landry had been the love of his life, until she showed up at his doorstep last night with his ring, an apology, and a suggestion he find someone else to go to the circus with. He should have thrown the damn tickets away, but perhaps the need for some sort of cheer—and the pervasive need to show Estelle exactly how much he didn't need her—had driven him to put on his good shoes and crawl out of the house with all the dignity he could muster.

Now he finds himself wandering to the lonely caravan. As a child he always loved the circus sideshow. He saw the dwarfs and the Siamese cow and the mermaid with the skin like salt. He tried his hand at the cards, had his fortune told, and stepped into the hall of mirrors. But there is no hall here, no glass case, no elaborate cloth tabletop. Heavy curtains hang over the entrance, smelling of a husky sweetness. He pushes them aside and steps through.

To his surprise he finds Estelle sitting by the window, her face still painfully lovely in the cloudless moonlight. Her hair falls in pale ringlets over her shoulders. She is wearing the scarlet dress and on her finger glitters the ring, though hazily he remembers throwing it in the river.

"Hello, Peter," she says softly.

He understands then, that this is not Estelle. Yet as she comes towards him, floating and light, that certainty evaporates. He teeters before this Estelle-not-Estelle. "You look so beautiful," he says hoarsely, truthfully. For she always does, in that dress. Before he can help it, he cries, "Estelle, why? You have to at least tell me why."

"Does it matter?" Estelle replies, ever so gently. She cups his face and he wants to sob with the familiar touch of her fingers.

"One last kiss," he begs. "That's all."

She leans in and touches her lips to his. Her mouth is soft and tastes of the sweet tea she brews every morning. He wants to drink in the scent, to hold onto this moment forever so it never ends, but Estelle draws back and once again she is lost. Except this time there is no biting turn, no cryptic sorry. This time Estelle looks at him with all the anguish he feels and she is not leaving.

This time he leaves. He turns and runs and pushes through the curtains, tumbling out into the hot night. The tears dry on his cheeks. He digs out the tickets from his pocket, one torn and one untorn, and holds them up to the wind. They flutter in the breeze and then catch, swelling like sails and lifting off from his fingertips, disappearing into the night like twin butterflies.

***

The Mirror of Longing knows her customers' deepest aches. They have the most troubled souls, the ones that are drawn to her, the ones that leave the big top still with a hole in their hearts. She steals them from the dissatisfying spectacle into the shadow of her embrace. Never the same. She can sense their desires like a desolate song, echoing through the night to her. The response that she sings, a harmony to every note of their loneliness, pulls them up her steps. The circus shows them all the things they have never seen; she shows them the things they want to see again.

For sad, grey-eyed Laura, she is a flutter of silver butterflies that flit about the darkest corners and take flight from the tip of Laura's nose. Her wings release a shimmering rain that makes Laura smile and twirl upon the rug. She reminds Laura of twilight in a forest glen, once in a happier time, where the stars shone like crystals and the fairies danced upon the leaves.

For the old bard Charles, who is going deaf in one ear and whose brittle fingers can no longer play his guitar, she is the song he has spent his whole life trying to find. She is flute and strings and rushing river, drums and harp and racing pulse. Every note is a snapshot of his youth, spent travelling across the country riling up crowds, no father and no lord, only him and his song. Each chord speaks of lyrics scrawled in fading ink by candlelight, calloused fingers plucking at the strings, and the echo of playing to the mountains. When the coda comes, Charles weeps.

For Nathan, who has never left his father's farm, she becomes the world he longs to see. The four walls of her wagon are the Omsbur Mountains of the Great White Way, their jagged diamond peaks trapped in spinning snow; they are the plunging ravines of the Fernel River, the blue vein of the South, flooding life into green fields and fishing villages, wildebeest herds and verdant forests. The ripples in the rug, which she purchased in a town's market for a cheap price because the pattern had been woven wrong, become the glittering Auran Sea, cobalt from one horizon to the other, cresting with white underneath an empty sky, or the undulating umber dunes of the Uncor Desert. The twisted lamp, which never holds its light, becomes the statue of Jorian the Chainbreaker, standing at the gates of the marble city of High Paravel with a spear in one hand and the shattered links held aloft in the other with ten thousand flowers planted at his feet for every slave whose shackles he freed. She herself is a proud freeman of High Paravel; a dark-eyed, supple limbed dancer of the Gjsela Tower, clad in skirts like streaming smoke and bangles cut from stars; a square-shouldered knight of the Blue King's army; a wrinkled fishmonger whose wrists are brittle but can still cut the vein from pale shrimps quicker than any youth.

She is all. Phantom mothers, won battles, recovered treasures. For Sophie, a clockmaker whose initials are carved into her family's timepiece. For Alex, a lost love, dark curls and burnt freckles. For Ari, a kind father. For Ezra, a better version of themself. It is the same in every city. Those townspeople who are content drift by her wagon without notice. They wonder, briefly, what it is the troubled folks find in there that makes them come out dizzy and sobbing, but these have always been the whims of troubled people, and besides, the wagon itself is so nondescript they are sure it contains nothing of any interest to them. There are brighter, more wondrous things to see.

***

She has spent so long being everything she has almost forgotten who it is to be nothing. But the memories are there, tucked away beneath the illusions, a younger woman with her own longing waiting for the circus to come to town.

She was the daughter of mirrormakers and through her father's steady hand and her mother's careful discipline she learned to polish reflections to a shine, learned to lay refractions in gilded frames so beautiful the passers-by could not help but be entranced by what they saw. She learned the angles at which the mirror could be set, just so, to show the customer what they wanted to see.

The ringmaster had come into their shop, just a simple man then, with dreams as big as any other customer. He was tall and thin and wore a dark coat with a split tail. She thought perhaps he would want to see himself as a more muscular man, with a straighter back and richer colours. But he waved off her attempts to place the right mirror.

"I want to buy all the mirrors you have," he said.

Her father brushed her out of the way, quick to spot an

opportunity. "All?" He hesitated, for he was really only asking to be polite. "Whatever for?"

"For my circus," the man-who-would-be-ringmaster declared, with a sweep of his arms. "I am putting together a circus, and every circus must have its hall of mirrors."

And so the mirrors went, stacked in the wagon, and in the gold came. She sat up and helped her parents count the coins, and as a reward they bought her a new dress and they ate the fattest cut of the freshest cow for dinner and she waited, with excitement, for the completed circus to come.

The carnival procession was grand and made the people cheer. The wagons in their bright colours paraded down the thoroughfare, the acrobats and the strongman and the fire-eaters waving, and the horses and the lions and the magician's doves stomping and roaring and fluttering.

She watched the big tent go up, and then the smaller ones for the strange things and the eclectic acts of the sideshows: the hooded woman with her glass ball, the wizened hag with her potions, the magician who proclaimed pick a card, any card. Most of all she watched for the hall of mirrors. It rolled in, in its own grand white caravan, its name painted in great letters on the side.

When night fell she ran to the carnival armed with her coins. The hooded woman cried, Your future! I see your future! And the wizened hag cried, Change your luck! No bad days from now on! And the magician cried, Pick a card, any card! But she ran past them all, right up the stairs into the hall of mirrors.

And there she found every single mirror smashed to pieces. The shards coated the floor in silver dust, reflecting fractals of the ceiling. In the planes that remained she saw a hundred splinters of her own horror, cracked along the edges.

Footsteps were coming up the steps, and she thought that she could not let this secret out. She spun on the stranger, a little boy with pink cheeks, and found she knew, without a word, what he was looking for. She drew from the splinters a thousand threads of a reflection and hung it in a gilded frame and turned it upon the boy, who saw in its sheen his dear dog who had died just the morning past. He leapt with joy and then wept and then dashed from her, both aching and swelled.

Another footfall threatened the stairs and she prepared the reflection, sensing out the want, but it was the ringmaster, freshly finished with his show. He had gained corded definition in his body since they had last met and he stood with cocky confidence and he wore a coat of red velvet. She found herself amazed, for she had been right.

The ringmaster surveyed the broken hall and said, "Would you like to join the circus?"

And how could she say no? The broken mirrors were swept and cleaned and she found herself a cot and a chair and a twisted lamp and a miswoven rug, and called it home.

***

It is the last day before the circus moves again. There is no true end to longing, but after a week in this field, where the wheels of the carnival wagons have begun to sink into the grass, she has tapered it to a trickle.

For little Lorelei, who builds palaces with broken sticks and painted murals on the walls of her bedroom before it burned down, she is a fine manor, a castle on a cliff, a glass spire, a great amphitheatre. Lorelei has a lightness to her step as she leaves, eyes full of replenished dreams.

Meanwhile she is...tired. It is usually like this, towards the end of another town. The first few days are a whirlwind of new visions and new aches. The stories she conjures touch her heart and she carries fragments of them, she knows, with her from town to town. Peter's Estelle will become a girl in some other boy's wonder; Charles' song a rhapsody in some other soul; Lorelei's palace the home of some other drifter. They are pieces of the same reflection, rearranged as needed.

For now she rests on her rickety rocking chair, gazing at her confines. Once pearly white, the walls have faded to a patchy cloudwash, the dark of the wood peeking through. They stopped in the famous pigment market in the Uncor Desert and the ring-master offered to buy her a fresh coat of paint, but she turned him down. She doesn't remember why. But she likes that there is something original in this room, something from when it was a hall of mirrors, and not just a tired woman.

The others—Nathalie the soothsayer, Great Heg the magician, even Jepp the top-spinner—they have come and gone. Moved on to other circuses, other exotic displays. Some have died. She alone has been the constant companion of the big top. She has seen the world, collecting its pieces, and shown it itself.

She senses a soul approaching and tunes into the longing. She senses apprehensive hope, the end of a long journey. A familiar shade of desire she can't quite place. Still she takes a breath and stretches for the threads, working on muscle memory now, bringing them together just as the newcomer steps through the curtain.

She becomes a young girl, with smooth skin and flowing hair and frayed edges on her best dress. The old woman that has entered stumbles when she sees her, eyes widening. "Guinevere?" she whispers. "Can it be?" The woman reaches for her laughing face, then draws back, and there is a shift in the longing like she has never felt.

"Oh, Guin," the old woman says sadly. "What have you done to yourself?"

She doesn't understand. Is there something wrong? She has never needed to second guess her instincts. She searches the woman's soul, finds the girl again, her nimble hands painting a frame. But the old woman shakes her head.

Frustration sweeps through her. She tries one more time: the girl standing in a doorway with a handful of coins. She runs through it, but stops, and turns, holding out a hand.

The old woman doesn't take it. "I don't want this, Guin," the woman says gently. "I thought I did. For many, many years I thought I did. I travelled all this way, wanting to see my little girl again. But now...show yourself, Guin. No more of these mirrors. Who are you?"

Who is she? What kind of question is that? Who does she want her to be? She probes that crack in the woman's soul and sees, in its deepest shadows, the flicker of a face. Triumphantly she grasps it and tugs, willing the new vision to spool about her.

Instead something slams into her chest and a consuming pain splinters across her, as though someone has taken a hammer to her ribs. She gasps; the woman catches her as her knees buckle.

"There you are," the woman whispers, and her eyes are full of tears.

Through the throbbing pain she smiles weakly, successful and satisfying. Whatever the old woman sees, it is a reflection she has not used in a very long time and its edges are cracked. Still, she thinks, cupping the old woman's cheek, because she senses it is what the woman needs, there is something strangely familiar about it, like an echo that has finally made its way back.

Leonardo's Children

Katerini Koraki

Katerini Koraki is the pen name of an author, reviewer, and lover of science fiction, fantasy, and horror. Her work has been published in Freeze Ray, Alternating Current, and Zimbell House, among other places. You can catch up with her on Instagram @Kreadseverything or on her website. She currently lives in New England.

As the circus ship landed at the dock of the recently established lumber planet, Leonardo was in the middle of his transformation from man to legend. He was well known, of course, or else the Titan Corporation would not have invited his circus to perform for their lumberjacks. But this was before the spectacle on Venus, before he became a bedtime story told to children so they'd dream of wondrous things. I will not be going into that story here. No, I bet you've heard that story a hundred times already. I bet you think of Leonardo as a dreamweaver, a demigod turning stardust to gold with his five beautiful children. No, I will not be focusing on Leonardo today. This story is not about my father. It's about the sixth child. It's about me.

From orbit, the planet Hathor looked like a patchwork quilt. Lush, deep green squares of just-terraformed pine forest stood stark against patches of razed land and wide, low buildings. I focused on the forest as our pilot lowered the *Big Top* down onto the landing dock. All of us were on the bridge, the six of us and our father. I met Avan's gaze across the room from my seat in the window, and shot him a cybernetic message. *Remember the days when you had to pilot the ship?* He didn't respond, just barked out a laugh and rolled his eyes. It always delighted me when he did that. Avan was the first of us to get an ocular implant and he was the master of rolling the natural one and the electronic one at the same time. Whenever Catriona tried to do that, her implant glitched and looked awful.

In the bright fluorescent lights of the bridge, I looked at Avan closely for the first time in a while. His skin had taken on a sallow tone, and wrinkles began to crawl over his face and left hand. Of course I knew that he was fifteen years older than I was, but it still shocked me to see the grey hairs peppering his beard. In my mind, Avan was always twenty-four, cracking jokes as he leaned back in the pilot's seat. Today, I supposed, he spent more time balancing the circus's accounts. I scanned my eyes over the perimeter of the room, examining each sibling individually. Each was different to my mental image, and with the amount of implants we all had, they were all starting to blend together. Leonardo, the last natural human left in our family, was in his quarters. He needed more sleep than any of us did.

A rough, bumpy landing stirred me out of my thoughts. The autopilot system played a prerecorded apology for any inconvenience, as if it didn't just shepherd us from one end of the Titan region to the other. In the pod next to me, Bell yawned and wiped the sleep from his eyes.

"What time is it planetside?" He asked as he made sure that his prosthetic limbs were still working properly.

"Three fifty two ma.m., TGST," The computer's voice chirped.

"Stars," Daphne breathed, "Let's hope these lumberjacks get up early."

Like children in the schoolyard, we all lined up outside the airlock doors. Age order, I noted, staring at the back of Elio's scarred, bald head. A loud wooshing sound filled the air and the doors opened. All six of us immediately felt a brick wall of humidity.

New terraforms were always the worst in terms of weather. Silently, I commanded my cybernetics to not go wonky on me. It didn't help that our father designed all of the implants in his ice-cold climate controlled lab, then dragged us all to perform on tropical planets. Most of the time, it didn't matter if something glitched out at a show. The audience was usually so stunned by what we were able to do that they didn't notice when things didn't go as planned. But this show was different.

There could be no margin of error. Perfection was the only option.

Just before Avan stepped outside of the *Big Top*, a door clicked open behind us. Wearing his signature crisp recreation of a red eighteenth-century military jacket, Dad strode to the front of the line and made sure he was the first to step foot on Hathor. He was the face of the circus, not Avan. It was his job to lead. Of course, none of that mattered when he slept for fifteen hours and left us to manage every task behind the spectacle. But when people were watching, Dad never let his mask slip.

A thin, white-coated person took our temperatures one by one as we stepped off the ship. About two or three months previously, a particularly bad outbreak of Venusian Flu ravaged the lumberjacks of Hathor. Titan lost a third of their expected lumber output for the quarter. They could not have that again, not when their buyers were clamoring for more wood to floor the new housing developments in the Fife Region. So, in somewhat of a farce, all of us cyborgs stood under the scope of a thermometer, as if we didn't have nanotech implants ensuring our immune system was perfectly functional at all times. Afterwards, the lumberjack, named Francis, herded us through a forested path to a concrete building. The dormitory for all human life on Hathor.

To our left as we walked in, the lumberjacks huddled around a thin space heater with a video of a fire playing on its screen. As

Francis' keys jangled in the door, all twenty of them in the sitting area whipped their heads towards us. The faces of the workers ran the gamut of emotions from friendly interest to disgust, almost horror. Francis flashed them all a warning look. Most of them looked away. A Siphonian in the back corner, though, spit onto the ground as soon as my siblings walked through the door. They didn't break eye contact with Avan the entire time. Bell, always the impulsive one, started storming forward, but Avan and Elio both restrained him.

Maybe we should have you walk in first, with your hair and single face mod, pretty girl, Catriona messaged.

Involuntarily, I touched the metal implant protruding from my ear. I pictured the leering eyes of the lumberjacks raking their way across my body and sat in my gratitude of being able to hide behind my brothers. The cold metal inside of my body, though, sat like lead as I swallowed hard. Just because most of my mods were internal doesn't mean I wasn't a cyborg. Even today, I can still feel the titanium vein running down my esophagus, the zirconium in my teeth and palate. I looked over at mostly-metal Catriona and shuddered knowing how much a night with her would go for on some planets. Once Francis showed us to our rooms, I shoved those thoughts away.

One of the most important parts of the Great Circus's rider was that each performer got our own room. It's true in any big family that things go smoother if everyone has their own space. That rule applies tenfold when that family trains and performs together. I slipped into my room, a tiny dormer barely bigger than my closet on the ship, and set my duffel bag on the table. The air in here was cool, and my window looked out onto a seemingly endless forest of pine trees. I wondered how long you could walk into it before you hit another razed patch.

I hung up my costume, packed away my extra clothes, and set out my makeup in front of the mirror. Carefully, I thumbed the only thing left in the bag. Before taking it out, I poked my head out the door to make sure no one would barge in on me. Of course they wouldn't. Father was still hungover and the rest of the family would sleep and charge what they needed to before rehearsal began in the evening. I twisted the lock shut, then pulled out my prized possession.

The little green glass bird shone in the electric light. I turned it around and around in my hands, watching the way the inside of the owl looked different at each angle. Smooth, cool glass met my fingers and I smiled. This was for me, all mine. I stole it myself from Mother's vanity before she disappeared and Father turned her room into another laboratory. As far as I knew, the owl wasn't important to her, just another piece of clutter on the countertop. Everything important had been shoved into the suitcase she took when she ran away, of course. But the owl still reminded me of her. At the same time, the ache in my chest for her now-vanished kindness only deepened whenever I looked at it. Daring to risk Father's ire if he entered and saw it, I placed the bird on top of the dresser and settled into bed.

My dreams, as always, were a twisted retelling of the circus. A wall of faceless audience members surrounded me and my family as we stood in the center of the ring. On an impossibly tall pedestal in the center, my father stood, clad in his vibrant uniform, narrating everything that was going on. To my left, Bell contorted his body into shapes inconceivable for any human. To my right, Catriona shifted her mechanical face into celebrities, cycling through the most beautiful people in this region of the galaxy. Above me, Elio and Daphne swung and jumped through the trapeze routine, arms and legs programmed to never miss the bar. Although I couldn't see their faces, the roar of the crowd grew louder and louder. I clawed at my ears, searching for a way to block the sound.

Then, suddenly, the ground beneath me started to lift. As I rose into the air, the crowd roar grew to a wall of noise. The big top collapsed as I rocketed into the sky, soon stories above the rest of the circus. I stared over the dizzying precipice, knowing what I had to do. What they expected of me. The titanium liner down my throat weighed me down as I attempted to calm my breathing. Frantic, I tried to figure out a way to get down. A loud crack from behind me jolted me back into the moment. I spun around on my toes and came face to face with my father.

His wild-eyed smile cracked his face open. "It's time, Fiona. My greatest trick. My greatest achievement. You are truly the improvement of the other models. Show them what you can do. Show them my masterwork."

I could feel it, then, the burning travelling up my esophagus. It started in the pit of my stomach, then shot its way up to my mouth. This wasn't how I practiced it. This wasn't how it was supposed to go. I was supposed to be able to control it, to lead the fire up through my body. Not be a sitting duck as it ravaged whatever organs it could touch. It took all my energy not to double over in pain, to clench my jaw shut and see through the tears welling up in my eyes. My father's laughter rang out as my muscles gave in and the fire, white-hot, erupted out of my mouth. *The Dragon Girl,* he shouted. The dream continued as I burned to death on the podium, listening to the deafening cheer of the audience.

Sweat soaked my clothes and sheets as I woke up back in the dorm room. I forced my pulse to calm down as I stared at the white cinderblock walls. When I could move steadily again, I glanced over at the clock on the end table. Four PM. I almost never slept for such a long time. It didn't matter, though, because I would never be able to go back to bed after that nightmare. It was time, it seemed, for a walk in the woods.

Except I didn't actually go to the woods. Not that I was ever near it, but I tended to stay away from nature back then. Something about it just felt unsettling, desperately foreign to me. Today when I'm planetside, I enjoy some wild beauty, but back then, I wouldn't be caught dead alone in the woods. So I walked away from the woods, back into the lit-up plaza of the lumberjacks' buildings. Off in a field in the distance, I could see the droids lifting up the big top tent. The candy-striped behemoth seemed to inflate, towering above the nearby trees. I turned away from that, too, towards the building next to the dorms: the lumberjacks' bar. Technically, it was a cafeteria, but from what I could see, there was no food and a giant shelf full of alcohol.

Luckily, at this point in the day, most of the workers were still out in the woods. Inside was the same whitewashed cinderblock room, except this time with a mahogany bar near the left wall. Only one person sat at the bar. It was a thin, pale human, with short red hair and a sunken face. He sported a uniform- the first one I'd seen since arrival. Much like the architecture, it was a bland, beige jumpsuit with the TitanCorp logo emblazoned on the right breast pocket. Briefly, I debated turning around and going somewhere I could be alone. Then, I remembered how much I needed a stiff drink, so instead, I took a seat next to him.

For a minute, he just stared at me, taking it all in. His eyes drifted over the metal bar coming out of my left ear, the long black braid I inherited from my mother, the cybernetic sparkle in my eyes. Unlike the men before, he didn't look disgusted. Just mildly interested. Up close, I could see the deep bags under his eyes and how his hair hung limp to his shoulders.

"What do I have to do to get a drink around here?" My voice came out husky and dry from weeks of disuse.

The man's eyes flicked back to mine. "Just go over there and grab one yourself."

I froze at the sound of his accent. He wasn't human. Sensing my shock, he chuckled and lifted up his hair to reveal the silvery scales on the side of his neck. He was a Jada. A telepath and an empath.

Which means he could feel my misery.

"My name is Rory. It's nice to meet you, Fiona. Usually, I have trouble reading modded people, but your emotions are strong. I hope you enjoy your time on Hathor and find the answers you seek." Like all Jada, his voice was smooth and soothing. I didn't let that bring my guard down.

"Oh yeah? Have you found answers here yet, Rory?" I snatched a can of beer from the collection and started drinking.

His eyes darkened. "No. I haven't found anything."

At that point, Rory looked genuinely upset. We sat in silence for a while, nursing our drinks. Alcohol felt like nothing to me compared to what I was used to. Every few moments, I'd spare a glance in his direction and find him despondent, staring into space. Emotions like that always made me uncomfortable. So I spoke up.

"Why are you here, then? If it's doing nothing for you? I thought Jada are supposed to be, like, super spiritual or whatever. One with the universe."

Rory turned his head back to me, locking eyes. When, after a few moments, I still waited for him to respond, he spoke again. "So your father didn't tell you, then?"

"Tell me what?"

A humorless grin spread across his face. "Hathor is effectively a prison planet. We're all working off our debts to Titan."

I sat with that idea, stunned. Of course, I knew about the Titan Corporation's business practices. Father held them over our heads the minute any one of us complained. A life in the circus wasn't perfect, he reasoned, but it was certainly better than wage slavery under Titan Corp. Still, the way Avan and he had described Hathor was as some sort of pastoral idyll. I supposed he wouldn't talk trash about the crowds buying peanuts and tickets. I visibly froze. Rory went easy on me after that.

"It's not your fault. They don't tell anyone about the bad parts, just how noble and beautiful it is to work as a lumberjack. As if we just hike around and cut down trees at random. When the reality is the opposite. Did you know that lumberjacks are the most likely to die at work? It's true. I read it a few years ago in a science magazine. Before I started here, obviously."

I almost smiled at that. We could relate to each other more than I suspected. Even though I'm sure he could read my thoughts, I went out on a limb, anyway, to see if we were as similar as I thought they were.

"Do you think about leaving, ever? Just stealing a pod and getting as far away as you can on a fuel tank?" I didn't even look at him until I finished the sentence.

He was silent for a moment, looking down into the deep amber of his glass. "Of course I do. I dream about it all the time."

With that, I trusted him completely. He knew the simmering terror of confinement as intimately as I did. We were twins in sorrow. The rest of the conversation we had in our minds, if you could even call it a conversation. It wasn't an exchange of words or ideas, it was greater than that. Somehow, Rory and I became of one mind. Thoughts, feelings, and concepts bubbled up organically, and no words were necessary to assess them. He entered my inner monologue.

By the end of half an hour, we'd hatched a plan. In my mind, there were just urges pulling me towards what I had to do and images of a potential future. My pulse raced like a hummingbird as I stepped out of the bar, feeling Rory's eyes boring into the back of my neck. Quickly, I checked the watch embedded under the skin of my wrist. Time enough to do what I needed to do.

Objectively, I knew that sneaking around the dorm on my tiptoes would raise suspicion from my siblings, who would be awake and readying themselves for rehearsal at this point. Still, I tried to be as light on my feet as possible as I made my way up the stairs and back into my room. As I placed object after object into the duffel bag, I sat in my disbelief. I wouldn't quite grasp what I was doing until later on in the night, far away from Hathor. In the packing stage, it all still felt like an elaborate prank fueled by the hysteria rising in my chest. Before long, all that was left was my costume and the owl.

The metallic, glittering costume was obviously not coming with me. The skin over my ribs grew goosebumps at the sheer thought of the tight, rough fabric. I wondered what Father would do with it after I was gone. Thinking of it now, I bet he just had Avan dispose of it somehow. Most likely, Avan threw it in a dumpster on Hathor or burned it. The irony of the latter option isn't lost on me. But I like to think that Avan kept my costume. That he keeps it hidden somewhere in the back of his closet and runs his hand over the gold glitter to remember me.

But I have very little time for such thoughts.

As always, the last item to join me was the owl. I ran my fingers over its smooth planes again and tucked it gently into my pocket. Finished, I stared at myself in the mirror and tried to even out my breath. Then, I walked out of my room for the very last time.

The universe tends to laugh at my plans. This time was no exception. The moment I stepped foot out my door, I was greeted by Daphne. She was the most visually distinctive of my brothers and sisters due to her rose gold prosthetics. Everyone else got plain black. Daphne was clearly on her way back from the bathroom, a yawn running through her frame. The visor that had replaced her eyes gave me a quick scan, then she smiled. A moment later, she saw the bag in my hands and confusion spread across her face.

"What's going on, Fiona?" Her voice came out clear, like the ring of a bell.

Any words died in my throat. I couldn't think of an excuse to explain the bag away on the spot. Instead, I chose to change the subject. If I couldn't tell her my plans, I could at least be a little bit honest with her. I could give her a crumb of the genuine love I felt for the sister I hoped to never see again.

"Here, I got something for you." I reached out and folded the little owl into her hands.

Daphne glanced up at me, then back down at the owl. "It's so beautiful! But...where could you have possibly gotten this? And why are you giving it to me now?"

I hitched the bag further up on my shoulder and hoped she could see the desperation in my eyes. After a few more seconds, it clicked. Daphne's entire body stiffened. She shifted her weight between her two feet, conflicted over whether to run to Father's room or stay where she was. Her tongue moved against her teeth as she tried to figure out what to say. As for me, guilt weighed down my body. I really put her in an impossible situation.

"Please," I intoned, "If I do this, then you'll know that you can too, someday."

Her lips formed a tight line as she surveyed me up and down. Then, after an eternity, she nodded. My muscles relaxed as I threw my arms around her, the metal of her limbs cool to my touch. I pressed the owl into her palm again before rushing out of the building.

I did not look back.

Deep in the woods was a clearing. Not a patch of deforestation, with stumps coming out of the ground like zombie fingers, but an actual clearing. Further ahead was a large hangar with plenty of small spacecraft designed for short-term travel. There were a few earth scientists on Hathor, Rory explained, who wanted to study the effects of controlled deforestation on a newly terraformed atmosphere. They needed these ships in order to complete their research. Practically, they never left Hathor's orbit.

Theoretically, they could make it to Buri, a large nearby planet that saw plenty of traffic and kept very lax records.

I shivered in the cool of the forest sunset and waited. With each moment, I lost a little more hope. Maybe Rory was just joking. Or, worse, maybe he was hired by Father to see who would even consider leaving the Great Circus. Nausea took over my body as

I thought of that being true. I would never see the light of day again. He would take away my eyes, this time, or my heart. Just as I was about to sprint back to the tent, though, I saw a red-headed figure come out from between the trees with a carabiner full of keys in his hand.

You're early. This bodes well for our journey, he messaged.

I let out a wild laugh. *I can't believe this is happening.*

He walked to the hangar and opened one of the large doors. I looked around the clearing to make sure no one was watching us. *Come,* he messaged.

I slipped into the dark hangar to find, as I expected, a line of small spacecraft. Lining the walls of the hangar were counters covered in tools and equipment. Rory grabbed a canister of fuel off of the wall and inserted it into the spacecraft. A silver pair of scissors glinted in the fading light and, once again, I knew what I had to do.

Wait. I just have one last thing to do first.

Summoning all the strength in my body, I grasped the implant on the side of my head and pulled. Intense pain blossomed in my ear canal, but I pushed through. Once I was able to jam it out far enough to expose the wires, I took the scissors in my shaking hand and cut them off. For a moment, my vision blacked out and blood rushed to my head. Then, slowly, the hangar came back into focus. When I came to, I was leaning on the counter, grasping it with white knuckles. Blessed silence returned to my body.

It was done. The first cybernetic addition, the one that "cured" me of the way I was born and taught my father to play God with our bodies, lay discarded in the dirt at my feet. I looked up towards Rory and smiled. Now I could start to be myself again.

The ones inside will go next, I said, nothing short of gleeful.

Rory just kept my gaze then, eyes sparkling. Without speaking or even telepathy, he opened the door to the shuttlecraft and slid into the pilot's seat. For a few moments, I stood and let the joy wash over me. Then, I got in next to him.

Are you ready for this? I asked.

I've been dreaming about this moment forever, I think . He responded, almost instantly.

Me too. Now let's go before they get the chance to shoot us down.

With that, he revved up the engine and we lifted off, into the infinite ocean of the sky. As far as I know, neither of us have ever been seen again. And I hope we never will be.

Of Moonlight and Music

Kayla Whittle

Kayla Whittle is a marketing coordinator currently working for a medical publisher in New Jersey. "Of Moonlight and Magic" is her first published work. She can be found most often on Instagram @ caughtbetweenthepages and on twitter @kaylawhitwrites.

Every full moon, the circus arrived and overtook the clearing in the woods while those in the nearby village ignored it. Locked in their little wooden houses bordered by pretty gardens, curtains pulled tight over their windows, the villagers told stories to cover the noise of footsteps. Strangers made their way down narrow lanes, across the wide square, walking into the woods. They kept to themselves; they kept quiet, never disturbing the fragile peace the villagers stole for themselves.

In the morning, those strangers came stumbling from the trees, blinking in wonder at mediocre fields. Feet bare, mud crusting around their ankles, they never lingered long and were always polite when they asked for directions back to the village. In the square, strangers shuffled between stalls of goods, handmade and precious. Jars of jams and miniature painted dolls, flower crowns woven from the pink and blue buds grown at the edges of their fields. The doors of the bakery were propped open, the scent of rising bread and spun sugar spilling out over the cobblestones.

The strangers' hands shook as they paid for a meal. Their footsteps were uncertain when they sought after the cobbler to cover their scratched and bruised feet. By nightfall, all strangers were gone. They spent their money well, but the villagers never tried to speak with them. Those who were drawn to the circus couldn't speak of the things they saw in the woods.

Each full moon was the same, until one arrived and Elsie Bartlow woke with starlight caught behind her eyelids. When she stretched and groaned, did her best to avoid properly greeting the day, Elsie glanced downward and saw pink, blushing flower petals circling her wrist. They weren't soft or sweet-smelling but unsettling, sitting flush against her skin, an unexpected tattoo. Picking at one of the petals with a sharp white nail, Elsie admitted to herself they were beautiful even as her skin stung with the pain of pressing too hard against her wrist.

Born in the village and likely to die there too, she knew this full moon she'd be going to the circus. She and her friends had often clung to the rumors adults never liked to acknowledge, thinking that speaking of the circus would draw its attention. Whispering, giggling, they'd placed wildflower petals on their skin and terrified each other with guesses at what went on at the circus. The strangers drawn to the woods always had flowers wrapped around their wrists, imprinted in their skin, a call to the circus that couldn't be ignored. The pull of magic would draw them to the woods just a short walk from Elsie's home, so she supposed in a way she was lucky. Those strangers would have had their petals appear days ago, their journeys already started.

Swinging her legs over the edge of her bed, Elsie nearly fell when she made to stand too quickly. Her thoughts dizzy, too disjointed to keep her properly grounded. Fast approaching twenty, Elsie had never learned to walk with much grace, something her mother kindly, consistently mentioned. The noise of her walk to the kitchen—all creaking floorboards and rattling picture frames—resulted in her mother waiting expectantly, already turned to greet her when Elsie stepped into the room. The heady scent of baking bread and roasting meat filled the space between them and began its small task of breaking Elsie's heart. Tucking her hands behind her back, she hid her wrist amid the folds of her nightgown.

"Good morning," her mother's smile already wavered uncertainly by the edges. Faint lines made their impression by her dark eyes and her hair had begun to gray at the roots. Suspicion raised an eyebrow as she took in Elsie's awkward stance. "What have you done now?"

Like most people who spent too much time alone together, Elsie and her mother couldn't hide much from one another. It'd been the two of them, just them, since Elsie's father died back when her age could still be counted in months.

"It will be all right," Elsie said, which was never a good sentence to begin with, but she believed it to be true. Most strangers returned from the circus, even if they were never quite the same or able to speak about the things they saw. The same magic that'd drawn petals on her skin, that would drag her into the woods if she tried avoiding the call, kept anyone from speaking about anything they saw after entering the tent.

It was terrifying and fascinating, and Elsie held up her wrist so the petals pressed around it nearly glowed in the sunlight streaming through the crooked kitchen window. Her mother gasped; they ended up burning the bread.

Their table was just the right size for two to sit without their knees knocking together underneath. Elsie and her mother drank strong tea, Elsie's teacup rattling against its saucer, as they sat and cried and tried to think of what to do.

"I must go," Elsie said. Those who resisted and tried to run, ignoring the warning on their skin, would be pulled to the woods as if by an invisible thread once the circus began. Strangers who listened and heeded and went into the woods once dusk turned to night had a chance of returning. Refusing meant Elsie would be taken anyway and she'd lose any opportunity to come back.

Her mother frowned, the lines around her eyes tensing, before she refilled Elsie's teacup.

"You'll go and then this will be done with," her mother said, or hoped. "No one in the village has been called before. The circus won't be wanting to keep you."

Elsie smothered her expression by taking another sip. The circus's call came with few guarantees.

The day's hours seemed too few. Elsie helped her mother clean and stack away the breakfast dishes; she settled her teacup next to her mother's, like any other morning. Then she tidied her bedroom, just in case, making her bed with a sense of finality that made her think of things long missed and all she had left to lose.

Her mother went to the town square, but Elsie didn't want to see anyone else. The villagers had always looked at her strangely for things that had happened before she could speak. Most of those girls she'd spent time with whispering around rumors of the circus had already made good on their threats to move away, running after something the village had been missing. Elsie loved her home, the dirt and cobblestone streets, faded flags hanging on street corners and bright festivals ushering in winter. Whenever she felt like a piece of herself had gone missing, a jarring hole temporarily plugged in her chest to keep her from sinking, Elsie never felt like leaving home would help her feel whole.

Sprawled out back in their pretty garden, framed by flowers she couldn't quite look at without feeling queasy, Elsie tried to memorize the sun and clouds and sky. Tried not to wrinkle her blue dress, her best one even if it was a little old. A ladybug landed on her outstretched palm, lingering there. When it walked, tracing the lines in her skin, it tickled and made Elsie want to cry.

There was no time for it; day drooped toward dusk. Her mother returned with fruit-stuffed pastries from the bakery and the makings of Elsie's favorite meal, a stew she usually had the opportunity to taste only at birthdays and the new year.

"You'll need your strength for tonight," her mother said, pausing to touch Elsie's cheek as they worked side-by-side in the kitchen. The world had done a wonderful job reminding her of all the reasons she had to stay behind. "No matter what happens."

They ate mostly in silence, emotions too tangled and taut for the words to come out quite right. As the sun began to set, strangers stirred on the path leading through the village. Their forms backlit by pink and orange and gold.

When Elsie opened her door, the other homes in the village were shut tight. The villagers' attention turned inward, away, as she stepped over the threshold. Something tugged at her wrist, but it was only her mother pulling her back for another embrace.

"I love you." Her mother's voice was soft warmth and home, kindness and worry, eyes shining like the moonlight swiftly approaching.

"I love you, too," Elsie said, and she longed to assure her mother she'd return in the morning but didn't want to risk her final words being a lie.

Elsie's footsteps were silent as she went to join the crowd of strangers heading toward the wood. Earlier, she'd tried to insist on practical boots, the kind good for running and kicking. But her mother had returned from the market with softer shoes, black and silky, meant for dancing. Spinning on one heel, Elsie craned her neck, saw her mother rooted in their doorway to watch her leave.

That meant Elsie needed to be strong and couldn't cry, at least not until she was hidden in the woods. Strangers pressed close around her, unwashed and travel-worn, shoulders limp and wrists bared. A veritable garden of different blooms spread on their skin. Few of the strangers seemed eager; most were nervous, refusing to meet her gaze.

Cool air held her tight once she stepped beneath the trees. Little fingers of moonlight poked through the canopy, wriggling down to bathe her in stripes of silver.

The closest she'd ever come to the clearing was the edge of the fields, where the grasses grew wild and the other girls had tricked each other, claiming to hear the fading echo of the circus in the faraway trees. If she listened close, Elsie heard music—gripping, ethereal music—picking over the noise of so many feet crunching through brush. The notes were fragile, reminding Elsie of long-ago nights when her dreams couldn't still long enough for her to sleep and her mother would whisper lullabies like prayers.

Her new shoes grew muddy around the edges before Elsie reached the clearing. The trees parted, branches bowing aside, until a massive tent loomed before her. The fabric looked heavy, gleaming white as the moon hanging low overhead. Flags coated in snake scales fluttered on stakes driven into the dirt.

"Tickets, please." The call came softly but Elsie startled all the same. A rickety booth sat a handful of feet in front of the circus tent; each of those who arrived had to approach the man in the booth before entering. A long line formed by him, already winding back toward the trees. Elsie joined the end of the line, trying to decide what to do with her hands. She wanted to wring them, but didn't want to appear as nervous as she felt, and settled instead for wiping off the sweat on her blue dress.

In all the time she'd spent knowing she couldn't overreact or else risk worrying her mother, Elsie hadn't considered using a few minutes to worry about herself. Seeing the tent and the ticket-taker, hearing the music drifting from the open tent flaps, she felt a little sick. Somehow she doubted she'd be excused if she fainted there in the clearing. Elsie did with her unease what most villagers did with the circus: she ignored it.

"Where is your ticket?" the ticket-taker asked the boy in front of Elsie. When she caught the edge of the ticket-taker's smile, her nerves threatened to devour her whole. Although he looked quite nice in a well-fitted suit, scarlet rose pinned to his lapel, his teeth were sharp and eyes completely white, luminous like the moon above.

"I—I just—" the boy stammered and a sigh rattled in the man's throat when he saw the boy's bare wrists. "She—she shouldn't go alone—"

"No ticket," the man settled back into his booth. "No entry."

Some clung so tightly to those who'd been called they refused to realize they wouldn't be welcomed at the circus, picky about those it claimed.

Elsie blinked and the boy was gone. She looked forward, then behind her to the line stretched back among the trees—then to the ground, as if he'd fallen.

"Ticket, please," the man called to her, as Elsie realized she'd held up the line. The ticket-taker wasn't impatient; as she drew closer, the edges of that sharp smile looked kind. Lifting her wrist, Elsie turned to allow the man a good look at the petals embedded in her skin. "Thank you. Please enjoy the show."

When he gestured for her to go onward, Elsie's dainty shoes scuffed against the dirt. Her footsteps slow, reluctant, as she approached the tent. An impressive mural blossomed above the tent's entrance depicting a figure dressed in gold and silver and blue, gossamer wings spread across the surface, farther than Elsie could see.

"Thomas?" A woman with violets draped around her wrist peered into the faces of all who passed the ticket-taker, staring hard in the gloom. "Thomas, where are you?"

Elsie wondered if the boy had been sent outside of the woods or if the circus had decided to take him. Strangers politely brushed past her, having met the ticket-taker, deciding not to dawdle outside as she did. Some cheeks gleamed with dried tears; some eyes shone a little too brightly, though none had eyes like the ticket-taker. Drawing back her shoulders, pinching her cheeks, Elsie entered the tent.

Her mind sparked. It smelled like sugar, like the bakery in the village square, and flowers, freshly cut and overly perfumed. The musicians she'd heard stood just past the entrance, playing a tune she didn't know on instruments she didn't recognize. One glanced up and caught her eye before offering Elsie a wink. His eyes, like the ticket-taker's, like every other performer she could see, were pure white.

Servers passed with trays of multi-colored, steaming drinks or candies, spun sugar clouds clinging to sticks. Overhead, ropes strung among hoops as lithe figures in a rainbow of tight costumes walked and swung and dove between them. Unknown animals with curling ears and too many pairs of feet, dark as a slip of shadow, eased past at more than twice her height with performers hanging off their backs. Fire wavered and curved overhead, heat dripping down to caress Elsie's cheeks, following the careful ministrations of a woman balanced on one foot atop a stack of bookcases. Peering closer, Elsie realized she couldn't read any of the titles; the letters wavered on the spines, playing hide-and-seek with her gaze.

Taking a few steps forward, Elsie realized there was no floor to the tent; little puffs of dust and dirt followed the footsteps of those passing by. Patches of grass clumped at the bottom of the stack of bookcases, the heady scent of earth mixing with the perfume of performers who swept past wearing dark, beaded masks. No one working at the circus wore any shoes. Elsie's toes curled within her black dancing slippers.

Movement just in front of her nose startled her backward, until she realized it had only been an orange feather, fallen from a massive bird swooping overhead. The woman tossed a ball of fire upward, catching the bird. Flames licked, spread, devoured the creature until nothing was left behind. No, not nothing—a tiny sparrow flitted away, while strangers who'd gathered near Elsie applauded politely. Looking into the faces of those around her, the ones who'd been called to the circus, their expressions slackened, dazed. Her jaw tightened as she wondered if they saw the same things she did, or if perhaps the circus had managed to already encourage them to forget their fear.

Those invited to the circus had begun to spread themselves thin within the tent, to explore. Elsie walked onward, waving away each white-eyed server who approached with tiny cakes decorated to look like little suns, water in glasses shaped like swans.

One she hurried past, as the scent of baked apples reminded her of the pastries she'd shared with her mother just a few hours beforehand. She eyed stalls filled with dresses far more ornate than hers, skirts made of metal or petals or starlight. Some sold masks, dark and smiling or colorful and leering. Some advertised assistance on small painted signs.

See the future. The curtain hiding that stall billowed ominously.

Learn the past. A breeze drifted from the entrance, smelling like smoke and a hard day's work and the pang of someone missed.

Understand the present. Elsie frowned, brow wrinkling, because she didn't see an opening to that stall at all.

The circus was beautiful and wild and beginning to give her a headache. A few strangers still wandered the tent like Elsie, but most had gathered in the stalls or to watch the performances. They'd found the ways they fit inside the show. Pealing laughter outweighed the distress most had shown while entering the tent; the strangers around Elsie moved like they were caught in their dreams.

Elsie, however, sweated, nerves dialing up her heartbeat. Dabbing the back of her hand against her forehead, she tried to cut away from the bulk of the crowd. Past an orator with a woman's head and lion's body, past someone swinging a pocket watch, imploring those nearby to look into their eyes. Past a man with enormous, straining muscles, boosting strangers up to reach the trapeze high, high in the air.

Gripping her hands together so tightly she felt the hard lines of her bones beneath skin, the throb of her pulse, Elsie remained unmoored. Turning in place, she felt very lonely surrounded by the crowd. The strangers fixated on the circus as if unable to look away; the performers eyeing her from the corner of their eyes—though she hoped only her anxiety told her they watched her.

"Our show has something for everyone," a voice spoke over her shoulder. "There's no need for you to stand alone."

Ice dripped down Elsie's spine, a threadbare reminder of a faraway winter. Her gaze steadied on a performer, tall and confident, white eyes aglow, top hat set at an angle nearly too jaunty to survive against gravity. Hair dark enough to match the black jacket hugging her frame; lips a shade of pink that reminded Elsie of the flowers imprinted on her skin. The performer was beautiful; it did funny things to Elsie's heart and worse to her speech, so she thought it best to say nothing at all.

"I am the Ringmaster," the performer said while Elsie faltered and stared. "Are you not enjoying my show?"

"It's impressive," Elsie said, the words almost too loud and sudden. She thought of the ticket-taker and how the boy outside had disappeared because he hadn't belonged at the circus. Her hand tightened by her side, nails biting crescents into her palm. What if the Ringmaster did the same to those who didn't fit in, inside the tent? "It's . . . lovely."

Together they looked out over the organized chaos, sparkling costumes and bleary-eyed strangers, cackling performers, flowing drinks.

"Everyone comes to the circus to find something they've been missing. Those who leave are a little more whole, even if they can never explain to others what they experienced here," the Ringmaster said. As she spoke, Elsie's brow creased. There was a catch in the performer's voice—something like hesitation. As if she didn't know what to make of Elsie as much as Elsie didn't know what to do with herself.

"This doesn't happen to you often," Elsie guessed. It felt like she should apologize, when the Ringmaster's lips curved downward. Quiet for a moment together, Elsie felt a little like dying, so she cleared her throat to try to dispel her worries. "Does this mean you'll . . . you know."

"Do I?" the Ringmaster asked. Her eyebrow arched and it seemed the music played louder.

"The thing you all do," Elsie's voice dropped as if mentioning such a thing too loudly would mean her demise. She and her friends had thought up all sorts of horrible endings for those swallowed whole by the circus. "The people who come here and don't return."

The Ringmaster blinked slowly. For a being whose eyes were entirely blank starlight, it captivated Elsie how well her expression lent itself to derision.

"I told you everyone comes here for a reason. To find something that couldn't otherwise be given to them, out there," the Ringmaster said, gesturing with a vague flick of her hand toward the tent entrance Elsie could no longer see. They were in too deep. "Sometimes, that means keeping someone who'd like it better here than anywhere else. The people we keep are never unhappy about it. The ones they leave behind are the problem, I suppose. That's why we changed the magic of this place. Those who needed nothing from us were feeling left out, coming when they weren't invited. If our guests can't speak about what they see here, no outsiders will feel cheated."

Elsie watched the Ringmaster's dark curls swing as she shook her head. It felt easy to believe her, when the strangers around Elsie looked happy. A little enchanted around the edges, but their smiles genuine. Tears dried.

"Ringmaster?" Elsie hesitated, resisting the urge to chew on her lip. Remembering to pretend at confidence. "The outsiders don't feel, you know, less cheated. People feel a bit—I mean, most people seem to think—like you're killing people. Here. Something like that. Eating them, maybe."

The Ringmaster stared then as if Elsie had brought news of a recent death into the tent. "They think that?"

"A little bit," Elsie said, wanting to ease the information partially to save her own skin, and partly to make the Ringmaster stop looking so sad. "Yes."

"None of our visitors ever wander long enough to tell us such a thing." The Ringmaster sighed, adjusting one of the golden buttons on her jacket. With a sudden clap of her hands that startled Elsie, the Ringmaster started walking, gesturing for her to follow. "Come. You've arrived here for a reason, and our talk is wasting your night."

Seeing no other choice, and curious now that the Ringmaster seemed so thrown by Elsie's presence, she followed the Ringmaster deeper into the circus. They picked their way past sword swallowers and contortionists, a talking wolf, a mirror that showed another room and not the viewer's reflection. With each performance they passed, Elsie caught the Ringmaster watching her. Waiting for her attention to catch on something, captivated by something that would fill some void that'd supposedly been inside of her. When Elsie looked at the strangers who'd come to the circus with her, they seemed satisfied. Heads thrown back, eyes glazed over. Her skin itched; she rubbed her hands over her arms, uncomfortable despite the warmth trapped inside the tent.

The performances were nice, but Elsie didn't know what she searched for. Hadn't thought there had been anything missing within her to start with.

"Nothing?" the Ringmaster asked as they stepped aside to let a long-necked beast pass through. She waved for one of the nearby servers, toting a tray filled with small marshmallow houses, but Elsie shook her head at the offering. "There must be something for you here."

"I'm sorry," Elsie said, then frowned, because she truthfully didn't feel apologetic. She hadn't asked the circus to come calling. "I could just—"

"Please don't suggest you'll pretend to be interested in something. That isn't how any of this works," the Ringmaster said, pulling her top hat into her hands, turning it round and round by the brim. It sent a little spark of annoyance up Elsie's spine, that she had been forced to come to this place, and the Ringmaster was the one looking more uncomfortable.

"Ringmaster—" Elsie said, before her frustration got the best of her. "Do you have another name?"

The Ringmaster shook her head, curls flattened where they'd been pressed down by her hat. "Do humans often hold several titles?"

The reminder that these starry-eyed performers were something new, something different, didn't unsettle Elsie quite so much now that she knew she held an unusual position in the circus, too.

"Some do," she admitted. "I don't. I'm only Elsie."

"Only Elsie who refuses to behave like all the rest." The Ringmaster's pink lips pressed into a thin line. Her gaze shifted downward and Elsie shuffled her feet, but the hem of her blue dress was too short to hide her shoes. "Do you dance?"

"Occasionally," Elsie answered. "Not very well."

"I didn't ask that," the Ringmaster said. "Would you like to dance?"

Elsie glanced up toward the acrobats performing above them between clouds of smoke from the firebreathers. Listened close to the music drifting over the crowd.

"I would," she decided. "If you would dance with me."

Otherwise, she thought she'd melt into a puddle of nerves, if one of the other performers swept her up. The Ringmaster was tall and intimidating, captivating in a way that made Elsie forget herself, but she was the only one who'd approached Elsie there like she was someone worth seeing.

"I would," the Ringmaster agreed, and they strode through the crowd together.

Dancers whirled and dipped and swayed on a large, crowded makeshift dancefloor in the tent. The ground beneath their feet a carpet of soft grass. Performers lifted one another in convoluted, impossible contortions. Some led strangers around the floor, counting the steps for them aloud. The Ringmaster's gaze slipped from those dreaming faces to Elsie; the music swelled alongside Elsie's foolish heart.

Trying to seem at ease, Elsie couldn't remember how to appear relaxed, unsure what to do with her hands. Her palms were sweating.

"Have you changed your mind?" the Ringmaster asked, eyes narrowed. But her lips were quirked with amusement, so Elsie took her outstretched hand.

Neither truly led the other. The music swept them up, held them tight and close in the overwhelming heat. Elsie's shoes had been well-made and didn't pinch, nor did they make her stumble. For once she felt graceful, though no one back in her village would have ever used the word to describe her.

When the song ended, in the beats between that and the next, Elsie's nerves took hold of her lips.

"What is it like?" she asked. "To live here, always?"

"Wonderful," the Ringmaster said and Elsie saw her love, her pride in the circus, as she glanced around them. Then her head tipped aside, as she considered the question again, and added, "Lonely."

A new, brighter song began and they spun away with the crowd before Elsie could catch her breath to respond. But something had changed; something had shifted. When the music paused again, the Ringmaster leaned closer, and asked questions that had Elsie smiling wide, speaking about villages and cobblers and girls who left to see the world. When the music changed again, Elsie asked about circuses and performers, long days without a full moon.

The crowd of dancers around them thinned; Elsie's feet ached. The Ringmaster spun her, catching Elsie close in her arms. Close enough for Elsie to feel her sharp inhale, when the Ringmaster looked down to where their hands intertwined. The Ringmaster's fingertips drifted lower, tracing the blushing petals on Elsie's skin.

"It is you, then," the Ringmaster said, the two of them rooted in place as the last few couples spun around them. Reluctantly, the Ringmaster's grasp slipped away, hand hurrying to roll up the sleeve of her midnight jacket, tugging the fabric upward. Pink petals bloomed on the Ringmaster's skin. When Elsie pressed their wrists together, the blossoms were a perfect, unnatural match. "Sometimes even those of us already inside the circus have a need to find something, here."

It eased some of Elsie's anxiety, to find what had drawn her to the circus, but knowing the calling had been a person—someone tugged toward her as well—lit a glow within her chest that outrivaled the moonlight.

"You'll leave with me?" Elsie guessed—hoped, as the circus still did something terrible to her nerves—and took the Ringmaster's hand again.

"No," the Ringmaster said. "You will return home, because you aren't finished with your world yet. But I would have you return. To visit. If you'd like."

The music had stopped; the other dancers disappeared. Elsie thought of her mother and the village she loved, the heavy weight of something missing sitting heavy near her heart.

"Yes," Elsie decided, an answer that terrified and thrilled and sent her blushing all at once. "I would come back, if you called for me."

The Ringmaster offered her arm and Elsie tucked her hand around her elbow, over the rolled sleeve of her jacket. Together, they walked through the emptying tent, passing performers packing away gorgeous costumes, ropes lowering from the high ceiling. It felt like a long exhale.

"I hope you enjoyed your night," the Ringmaster said when they paused by the entrance to the tent.

"You were right," Elsie said. It was easy to ignore the other white-eyed performers, knowing they stared not so much at her but at their Ringmaster. "Your show has something for everyone."

Flushing furiously, she kissed the Ringmaster.

On the cheek. She was not feeling *so* bold, yet. The Ringmaster's smile lit between them like a soft moonbeam, as Elsie stepped out of the tent.

Blinding sunlight forced Elsie to squint and when she managed a glance over her shoulder, the circus was gone. Curling her toes in the dirt, Elsie—

Elsie realized her shoes were gone. She'd ask the Ringmaster about where they'd disappeared to, when the circus came again.

No strangers stood around her; the clearing in the woods was still. Hurrying through the trees, Elsie knew her mother would be worried, waiting. Wondering where her daughter had been taken during the night. Though Elsie wouldn't be able to explain what had happened because of the misguided magic that kept the events at the circus a secret, she knew she would answer when the circus came calling again.

Crab Pots

Amanda Baldeneaux

Amanda Baldeneaux is a writer based in Colorado.

The optometrist's office manager, Gwyn, made Skyla understand why men called phone sex hotlines. Gwyn whisper-spoke,
as though trying to keep her voice down so she wouldn't get in
trouble. It was the same voice Skyla's massage therapist used to
make her relax on the table. Gwyn's voice achieved the same
effect but without the incense, oils, and inflated tip. Skyla's tension headache softened as Gwyn told her that she didn't actually need to come in for an appointment to refill her contacts
prescription.

Outside, Skyla's two boys jumped and screamed on a trampoline, shoving each other into the protective netting. When Skyla
was a kid, there was no netting. The microwave timer beeped,
announcing that her pot of sugar wax for at-home bikini hair
removal had finished melting and was ready for ripping.

"I want to know if I'm a candidate for Lasik," Skyla said to Gwyn,
cradling the phone between her ear and her shoulder as she took
the wax bowl from the microwave. It sloshed over the side and
burned her finger. Skyla cussed to herself and slammed the
microwave door. Gwyn spoke again and Skyla inhaled, relaxing
like she did in yoga. "Yes," Skyla said, "I'm having trouble seeing
up close. I think I need bifocals. I want to fix the whole situation."

Skyla's husband had suggested she be assessed for Lasik surgery years ago, when Skyla couldn't wear contacts because they dried out her eyes, yet she refused to wear glasses except when she drove. She forgot them on her nightstand one day and rear ended an Uber driver on her way to work. She'd put up with the soft lenses ever since. The idea of Lasik scared her, but bifocals scared her more. Plus, she wanted to see what Gwyn looked like behind the kitten-soft voice on the phone. Skyla wished her husband could relax her a fraction as much.

"I can schedule you tomorrow," Gwyn said, drawing out her words. Skyla tried to picture Gwyn scanning the calendar on the computer for open dates as she spoke. She'd be wearing glasses—thin wire frames—her hair swept back into a ponytail as she leaned forward to read the small text better. Keys clicked in the background as Gwyn typed in dates. Skyla wished she could pay Gwyn to come over at night and talk in a library voice while typing nonsense onto a keyboard as Skyla fell asleep. Skyla couldn't sleep on her own anymore; instead she lay on her back and thought of everything she did do, didn't do, and needed to do that day and the next, her heart pounding harder as the lists stacked up.

Her fortieth birthday crouched just three weeks away. Her husband booked a cruise to the Caribbean for the occasion. He bought her a bikini. Skyla wasn't sure who he thought she was, buying her a bikini. She hadn't worn a swimsuit, let alone a two-piece, since before their first child was born eleven years ago. She'd eaten nothing but rice cakes and cottage cheese since he told her. She'd gone to Zumba in the afternoon before the kids came home from school and in the five minutes it took her to walk up the stairs she'd rip all of the hair out of the crepe-paper skin between her pelvis and legs. It'd be one thing if it were strangers who'd see her on the deck of the ship on the cruise, her body artfully draped in an overpriced caftan, but her husband had conspired with all of their couple friends, people they'd known since college, to come along, too.

Skyla could picture it, now. Everyone lifting a glass to toast her turning the big four-oh and having nothing to say about the life she had led. She'd left her career as a chemist to have her children. She'd become a woman who wore stretch pants and sweaters and Spanx. She put wrinkle cream that cost as much as their weekly food budget onto her skin every night, wondering if she'd look any different by this point if she hadn't. The crow's feet were still there.

Skyla agreed to the appointment time and hung up the phone. The wax box burned her hand as she set it onto the counter. She opened the kitchen window to yell at her boys to stop shoving each other on the trampoline.

"He's a lion!" the eleven-year-old yelled. "I'm a lion tamer!" He made a hoop with his arms for his brother to jump through.

Even on the weekend, she had to do all the parenting. Her husband had left for the afternoon to check crab pots with a fisherman friend, which was really an excuse to sit on the deck of a boat and drink beer with no shirt on. Whenever he went, he came home sunburned and had to soak in tomatoes for an hour, always staining the tub red for Skyla to scrub the next day.

"Yuck," she said, tearing a piece of paper towel and wiping the dead bees and flies off the tracks of the windowsill. The boys always left the screen door on the slider half open, and the bugs always found a way in but not out. Skyla crushed the curled bodies in the wadded towel and dropped them into the trash, noting that the flowers in the shrubs outside of the kitchen window looked wilted, and would need watering later. She had plant stakes in the garage; fertilizer always perked them up. She added the note to her mental to-do list. It was Sunday, and she never got much done on the weekend with the boys and her husband home in the house. Weekends always made her feel like a failure. The laundry didn't get put away; the dishes stacked up in the sink. No one would leave her alone long enough to go for a walk or a jog. In a few hours her husband would be home with a box of live crabs he'd ask her to butter and steam the next day, the crabs staring and snapping from their entrapment until the water boiled. If her family would just leave her alone she could get everything done without falling behind. She counted the number of years till her youngest left for college as she went up the stairs.

***

Gwyn did not look how Skyla had pictured her.

Skyla stood at the desk as Gwyn passed a clipboard over the counter for Skyla to update her insurance information for herself and the boys. Gwyn didn't wear glasses. She wore her hair loose. Strands of it fell into the gap of the oversized tank she wore beneath her V-neck blouse. Skyla tried not to stare. She'd always liked breasts. Breasts were far more interesting, to her, than no breasts at all, though she felt the same way about the presence of a penis versus a body without one. She sometimes wondered if she were bi and now, standing in front of Gwyn with the soothing voice and visible cleavage, Skyla wondered again. Skyla had girl friends who kissed each other at frat parties in college and at cheap bars in their twenties. They were married now, too, and still told stories about the "wild fun" they had in their heyday. Skyla had been there, but she hadn't been wild. Too nervous. Too shy. Her evangelical upbringing still hanging over her like a diving bell only she could see or feel. These same girl friends would be on the cruise and Skyla would bet all of the money in their healthcare savings plan that she'd hear these stories again over bottomless glasses of wine and piña coladas. Skyla wasn't sure why she was still friends with them; they'd been vapid in college, and were more so now, with their standing nail appointments and Barre-sculpted waists. All they ever talked about were their kids.

"All finished?" Gwyn asked, reaching for the clipboard.

Skyla signed her name and nodded. She handed it across the desk.

"It'll just be a few minutes," Gwyn said. She looked back at her computer.

Skyla rifled through the flyers for local businesses and events on the edge of the counter. She plucked one at random and pretended to read it to avoid sitting down.

"A circus," Skyla said, focusing on the words. "I didn't know those still existed."

"Unfortunately," Gwyn said, her voice lower than usual. She stopped her typing. "I mean." She reddened. "It has to be a lot of work. A traveling show."

"Especially this one," Skyla said. "They have mermaids. Can't imagine carting a saltwater tank across the country."

"It's not good for the mermaids," Gwyn said. "They don't live long in captivity."

"Like whales?" Skyla wanted to keep Gwyn talking. Gwyn's interest seemed piqued by the topic of circuses. Skyla wondered what else she was interested in. Bands? Art? Skyla had liked art once, though she couldn't name a single living artist. Skyla scanned Gwyn's hand for a ring.

"Any wild animal," Gwyn said. "I don't think they should be made to perform tricks for our entertainment."

"My grandfather used to say animals were like tomatoes; they don't feel anything if you pluck them from the vine. Weird, people used to think that way."

"Plenty still do," Gwyn said. Her shoulders tensed as she typed, but the pace of her entering slowed.

"You like animals?" Skyla asked.

Gwyn nodded. "I wanted to be a vet," she said.

"Why didn't you?"

Gwyn flushed again. "Didn't get in."

"I like animals," Skyla said. A half-truth. It was only true in the way that she didn't like to think about how animals were killed before she ate them. In her past life, she'd formulated cosmetics for a luxury brand and oversaw their testing on animals. Mostly rabbits. Some dogs. "I'm trying to teach my boys to be more compassionate toward other creatures. You know, stop stepping on bugs and throwing toys at the squirrels. Early toxic-masculinity stuff."

Gwyn's eyes darted side to side, but the doctor was in an exam room with another patient. She leaned forward. "There's a protest against the circus and its animal shows next weekend. If you wanted to expose your boys to activism, or animal rights groups, or something."

"Yeah," Skyla said. Full lie. "I'd love that."

Gwyn took out a notepad with the optometrist's logo on it and scribbled a number. She handed it to Skyla. "There's a planning meeting on Wednesday, if you can come. Text me and I'll send you the address. Sorry, I don't have it on me right now."

Skyla took the slip of paper with Gwyn's phone number. "I'll text you so you've got my number right now," she said.

***

The House of Cards, a boutique traveling circus, had set up on the county carnival grounds, a paved parking lot adjacent to a sliver of rocky beach and a pier that stretched over the ocean and ended in a bench-lined rotunda. Skyla had received one real text from Gwyn after the appointment. It stated the location and time of an organizing meeting for a local animal rights group, one made briefly famous for demonstrations against a casino that kept dolphins in an aquarium adjacent to the building's restaurant. Skyla's parents had taken her to eat at the restaurant when she was a kid. Her dad would play blackjack in the casino while Skyla pressed her nose to the glass of the dolphin pen and stuffed her belly with breadsticks 'till their meals arrived. She'd always meant to take her sons, but the dolphins had been released to a wildlife rescue group following the national attention drawn by the animal rights organization, and the aquarium filled instead with twenty-somethings in bikini tops and pull-on mermaid tails. Skyla hadn't heard how that venture was going since the discovery of real merpeople in the seas, but the humans in costume were probably better behaved than their authentic counterparts.

Skyla had tried to engage Gwyn in conversation through text, asking open-ended questions about the group and her involvement in it, but Gwyn had only responded with "yes," "no," and "maybe," until she went dark. She'd waved to Skyla from across the living room in a house that smelled like apple, cinnamon, and patchouli, but hadn't looked her way until Skyla raised her hand to volunteer for a job.

Skyla's husband had stayed late at work and the babysitter she'd hired to come to the evening meeting had cost almost as much per hour as Skyla made when she last worked in the lab. With Gwyn not even paying attention to her, the whole endeavor seemed like a bust. Not that Skyla was sure what the meeting would have looked like if it were successful. She'd heard of women who left their husbands for other women. Skyla wasn't sure why, but she imagined those women's new lives as freer than their old ones. No more designations of "his" and "hers." No more dirty socks balled up under the couch. No more pelvic pain when her uterus sat low in her body during sex. Once a woman cast off her husband for a female lover, what couldn't she do? People would wonder if she ever really loved her husband. They'd question everything they ever thought about her. Skyla liked the thought of everyone she knew wondering if they'd ever really known her; known even the most mundane details about who she really was. But then, Gwyn didn't say more than a cursory "Hello" until Skyla raised her hand.

Because she'd volunteered, Skyla now stood in front of the House of Cards ticket booth with her two sons. The group wanted observers to witness the animal shows before writing up an exposé of their treatment, to be followed by a protest in front of the circus gates the next day. The group leader had called it a "crab-pot strategy," gathering information to use against the circus so the employees would turn on each other when presented with evidence of animal abuse.

Skyla would take in the mermaid show, housed in a tent led by a ringmaster dubbed the "Queen of Cups." The circus had four primary tents, one for each queen and her suit in the tarot. A mole from the group would visit each. Skyla had hoped the position would be a team effort and that Gwyn might be her partner, but it was not and she was not.

"I want to see the lizards!"

"I want to see the birds!"

Skyla's boys tugged the circus's map back and forth between them. The Queen of Wands was a tent of reptiles, the Queen of Swords a tent of birds, the Queen of Pentacles a tent of mammals, and the Queen of Cups a tent of real, live mermaids. Carnival rides and games threaded between each tent, their blinking lights blurring as they competed for attention.

"You can each have twenty bucks," Skyla said, doling out money between them. "Five gets you into a show. The rest is for games and rides."

"Ice cream?" her nine-year-old asked.

"It's your money," she said. "Be back here in two hours."

The boys took off into the circus, tugging each other's shirts toward their preferred attractions before disappearing behind a funnel cake cart. Skyla checked the time on her phone. She'd called the circus two days before to request an interview with the showrunner of the mermaid tent and was referred to the Queen of Cups herself, a woman named Zania Peters. Skyla claimed to be from the local free weekly and hoped no one would call the editor to verify her employment. She was given a thirty-minute window with Zania in between showtimes; the next show started in ten minutes.

Skyla scanned her own copy of the House of Cards map to locate the Queen of Cups's tent. Close to the cliffs and the pier, of course. She was almost as interested in how a portable water tank worked as she was in seeing a real mermaid up close. She'd seen pictures of them, as had everyone in the world since their discovery five-or-so years back. They were not the replicas of humans that movies depicted, nor were they the manatees that mermaid sightings throughout history had often been dismissed as. They had humanoid faces; small jaws, a mix of pointed and flat teeth. They were kelp eaters, primarily—some fish and crustaceans—and had spent their years of undiscovery hiding amongst the thick kelp forests that anchored the sand and the sea into place along coastlines. They ate brittle stars and rockfish, and had perhaps single-handedly been the saviors of acres of kelp forest by bashing sea urchins on rocks to eat their soft insides, urchins that would otherwise have chewed through the kelp stalks at the root if left unattended.

The merpeople needed sunlight. They didn't tolerate temperatures that sharks, sport fish, or whales could. They clung to the shallows, relative for sea creatures, which explained so many sightings of mermaids on the rocks over the years. They lived in matrilineal colonies, with the females raising the young together and the males roaming and feeding alone. Their skin ranged from rust-red to green, perfect camouflage for the kelp forests they inhabited. Their hair, too, blended with the shades and shapes of the kelp so that if a merperson hid behind a giant stalk of kelp as a diver swam past, the diver would think only that the flick of a tail disappearing behind the stalk belonged to the fish, and the strands of hair and elongated limbs part of the kelp canopy's leaves. The females dug burrows into the sand, creating colonies like prairie dogs where the young could be hidden and raised to maturity. Mermaid tunnels had been found dug as much as a half-mile long, using the kelp roots as structural support for their homes. They begged the question of what else was still out there, unexplored or undiscovered.

Merpeople had lived only in labs until just a year or two before, then they began appearing in zoos. It took the first several years after discovery to learn how to build a habitat that would keep them alive in captivity for more than a few weeks. Some enterprises weren't interested in keeping them alive, though. Fashion houses wasted little time producing merskin purses, shoes, and belts. Even a sportscar had been made with merskin seats and an open top roof; the merleather was waterproof and ideal for all-weather travel. A few brave restaurants had put mermeat on the menu, though it was received about as well as grilling up a gorilla or endangered whale would be. Still, there were those with money who ate it. Skyla's research in the past few days prior had revealed that the House of Cards was the only circus that held mermaids (no mermen, as they couldn't be contained together) in captivity, successfully shuttling them from city to city to perform tricks like trained dolphins. Pictures and promotional videos weren't enough, though. Skyla wanted to see what a real mermaid looked like, face to face.

It hadn't been all interest in Gwyn's attention or curiosity about the appearance and behaviors of a new species that had driven Skyla to raise her hand at the meeting. She'd grown up on *The Little Mermaid, Splash,* and other depictions of mermaids as sexy sea vixens who sorcerers wanted to control and scientists wanted to cage. At least one of those things had come to pass. Everything Skyla had learned from movies as a child taught her that it was the good guy's role to free them. Skyla wanted to be the good guy; she spent enough time being told by her children that she was the bad guy. She made them do homework, eat spinach, go to bed, pick up toys. And that was after she left her job squirting eyeliner into the tear ducts of rabbits. Her husband only came home for dinner and bedtime, he didn't have to be the enforcer of rules. Her kids seemed to think she kept them in a cage of the house for her own amusement, but really, she just wanted to train them up as adults so she could free them and they wouldn't return. She dreaded the thought of her boys coming back to live in her basement like her brother-in-law did with his parents. There was no freedom with kids in the house. There wasn't much with a husband there, either, and maybe that's why she couldn't stop thinking of Gwyn. Gwyn, whose voice lowered her blood pressure, not raised it, like everyone else's.

Each ride and booth of the circus played music-box chimes that reminded Skyla of the boys' old exercise saucers from when they were babies. Whenever her husband wanted to have sex while the boys were awake—which was always—he'd set them in the bouncers and turn on their music so they'd stay quiet and contained on the other side of the room. Skyla still heard the toys' five second looped tunes in her head during sex.

She turned right at a Ferris wheel, forcing her mind to focus on the sounds of gears turning, carts creaking as they rocked back and forth in their cradle. Rocks crunching underfoot. Unpopped corn kernels crushed between teeth. Beneath it all, the rush of water against rocks just past the fence of the fair grounds. Seagulls. Wind flipping tent flaps back and forth, making them strain against their weighted stakes. Banners proclaiming the Queen of Cups Mermaid Show with jumbo pictures of a woman encrusted in seashells let Skyla know she'd found the right tent. She waited in the crowded line, then handed over the admission fee and was shuttled inside to risers encircling a round, plexiglass tank. The back half of the tank was hidden by submerged doors and an overhead curtain. A catwalk extended over the tank in a giant "X" and deep, baritone-driven music that effectively called up the deep sea played over the crowd. Skyla checked her phone again. No messages from the boys, and she'd made it to the show with just two minutes to spare. The House of Cards website had noted that the Queen of Cups show filled up faster than any of the other presentations on offer and encouraged attendees to arrive at least thirty minutes before each show time to get in line. Skyla was lucky it was early in the day, otherwise she probably wouldn't have made it in, and wouldn't have had anything regarding the show to ask about when she interviewed Zania Peters. She crossed and uncrossed her legs. She felt like a spy. She was a spy, she supposed. That would be something to talk about on the cruise, for sure.

Skyla shoved her phone in her pocket. The circus had a strict no filming policy, and the waiver she'd signed at admission had threatened to confiscate the phones of patrons who violated the rules. The overhead lights dimmed, and the music lowered. Smoke rolled across the water of the tank. Skyla instinctively leaned forward in her seat, eager. The doors in the tank slid open, but the mermaids jumped over them as though they weren't even there.

***

Skyla waited until the crowd had cleared and circus staff swept through the aisles with brooms, cleaning up spilled popcorn and lemonades before the next audience was ushered inside.

"You'll have to exit, ma'am," a staffer said.

"I have an interview with Zania Peters," Skyla said, standing. "I'm from the Free Weekly. She's expecting me now. Where do I find her?"

The teenager assessed her, leaning on the broom handle, before shrugging and jogging down the riser steps. He disappeared behind the tank, then reappeared minutes later, beckoning her with a single hand wave.

Skyla followed him around the tank and behind the curtain.

Past the tank's doors, the mermaids that had just performed swam languidly in a cluster on the other side of the tank. They were smaller than humans, but still larger up close than she had expected. They ignored the humans walking around their enclosure backstage as otters would in a zoo. The teen stopped in front of another curtain.

"Ms. Peters?" he called. "She's here." He nodded at Skyla and left.

The curtain swept open and the tent's ringmaster, the Queen of Cups, stood from a folding metal chair. Up close, Skyla saw the fabric of the Queen's pants were made from real merskin leather. The queen's makeup had the off-putting largesse of stage makeup seen at too-close range, the eyeliner too black and the lipstick too red. The woman smiled and held out her hand.

"Zania. First time seeing live mermaids?" she asked.

Skyla nodded. "I'm here to talk about you, though." A lie.

"Have a seat." Zania gestured at a folded chair leaning against the collapsible table. Skyla opened it and sat. She turned on her phone's recorder.

"You're nervous," Zania said. "New on the beat?"

"No." Another lie. "Sort of. I've mostly dealt with industry."

"I'm an empath," Zania said, crossing her legs. "I can read your emotions. It used to be part of my act, but audiences just wanted mermaids. Subtlety is a lost art, don't you think?"

"I suppose," Skyla said. Her mind spun and she opened the notes app on her phone to review the questions she'd prepared. The animal rights groups had instructed her to ask about the training and treatment of the mermaids, without being too direct. She was normally good at not being direct; she'd become a master at it in marriage.

"So, how does being an empath work? Is that like being a psychic?" Skyla asked.

Zania shook her head. "I can't tell the future," she said, smiling. "I just know what you're feeling right now, even if you don't."

"Interesting," Skyla said. Half-truth. She found it interesting a woman believed she could read emotions rather than the idea that someone actually could, which she couldn't. "Does that work by observation? Touch?" She wiggled her fingers in the air. "Auras?"

"Little of A, little of B," Zania said. "There's no exact science. I just get a sense from all interactions. Face time, touch. General air. How do our eyes interpret text?"

"I'm not a neuroscientist," Skyla said.

"You feel underappreciated in your work," Zania said. "Others don't see its value."

Skyla shrugged. "Journalism is tough, these days. When did you discover you had these...powers?"

Zania considered. "Since I was little. I touched my mother's skirt and knew she was going to leave my father. I could feel her unhappiness. She left him when I was eight."

"Do you feel what animals feel? Like when you wear leather?" Skyla pointed at the queen's merskin pants. "Does that help you connect to the mermaids you're training?"

Zania laughed. "I don't feel anything from animals," she said. "I don't believe we should anthropomorphize them. They act on instinct. Maternal instinct. Survival instinct. They don't feel sad or unappreciated and then scheme to run away from their den mates. That's one of the problems with mermaids; they were assigned human characteristics, feelings, and complexities long before their existence was even discovered. They came out of the water with all these expectations already heaped upon them. They're smart enough. Not dolphin-smart. But smarter than fish. Crabs. I wouldn't want one as a pet. They aren't cuddly. They're wild. They perform for food. As long as we feed them, they're happy."

"How did you acquire the mermaids in your show? It still surprises me that they evaded fishermen and divers for so many years."

Zania checked the time on a phone set face down on her table. "I caught them myself," she said. "They have a hierarchical system, much like whales or wolves. Any pack animal. It's part of why I wear their leather. I've trained them to see me as their alpha. It's why they do as I say. In addition to the food."

"How did you catch them?"

Zania smiled. "My grandfather dealt in skins. Dirty business, I know. But, that was the times. We lived down the coast near the wetlands. He used to catch nutria on the shore with large traps. Looked like oversized crab pots. He'd set them out during low tide and the rodents would go in for the bait and get caught. Water would rise and they'd drown in the cages. Kept the fur pristine. He died years ago, but my mother, she kept all his old traps in the garage. I was working down in Florida at a mermaid cove—the fake kind, with women in tails—people came from all over to see us swim around in pools with flowers and shells on. When real mermaids were found, business dropped and a bunch of girls were laid off. I knew I'd seen a real mermaid when I was a girl, but no one ever believed me. I got a few of my grandfather's traps and snapped them together to make a big one, wove kelp through the rungs and put some urchins inside, then set it out at low tide and waited for the water to come back in. Sure enough, a mermaid swum in, got herself stuck, and was stranded when the tide went back out. She died and I sold her skin for enough money to pay off my car. Once other people figured out how to catch them, though, prices went down. The real trick was catching one and keeping it alive. The females are easier to keep alive; they're heartier. I missed performing, too, so when I saw an add for an animal trainer with performance experience, I applied. Offered to catch and train my own mermaids, and here I am." Zania opened her arms wide.

"That's quite a story," Skyla said.

"You're jealous," the queen said. "It's more exciting than house-work, that's for sure."

Skyla squirmed. "I like my life," she said. A half-truth. "I like writing." A lie.

"It's alright," the queen said. "Everyone secretly wishes they could join a circus. Want to see the mermaids? I have twenty minutes." She stood.

Skyla followed the queen out of her dressing room into the back-stage of the tent. The mermaids swam together in circles around the enclosure. They could have been penguins in an aquarium, or seals. They swam round and round, amused or trapped, Skyla wasn't sure. She'd once heard goldfish had no memory, and each trip around their bowl a surprise. She wondered if that was true for the mermaids. Or, true enough. They could remember their routine. Backflips. Jump through hoops. Synchronized swim-ming. Lobbing volleyballs with their heads. Skyla had winced as their small breasts bounced up and down with each jump; she was surprised the circus hadn't outfitted them with bikini tops, though the near-human nudity of it was probably an enticement for many.

Zania led Skyla up a flight of steps to the edge of the tank. She picked up a bucket of kelp strands and dangled one over the tank. A mermaid launched herself out of the water and took the kelp from Zania's hand before splashing down again.

"Want to try?" Zania asked. She stuck her hand in the bucket of brown soup and brought out a rubbery strand.

Skyla nodded, taking it. She held the kelp with the tips of her fingers and tensed. Two mermaids jumped up, vying for the treat. One latched the kelp with her teeth and yanked it out of Skyla's hand before disappearing back into the water and across the tank.

"You're ready for showbusiness," Zania said.

"As long as I wouldn't have to scrub the tank," Skyla said.

"I don't do that," Zania said. "Someone else hoses it down before we leave."

"What do the mermaids travel in?"

"Glorified bathtubs," Zania said. "We give them a mild sedative and keep them submerged until we get to the next city. It takes about a day to set up and fill the tanks, and then we wake them up, shake them up, and put them back in. They don't even know they've traveled."

Mermaids who hadn't received treats began to congregate beneath the platform, crowding each other as they vied for space beneath the two women. They opened and closed their mouths expectantly. Their eyes were disconcertingly human, though rounder and farther apart, like a fish. They had tiny, barely formed noses that Skyla had read functioned solely for sniffing out food and predators rather than breathing. Their gills, like other fish, were slitted over their ribs. They were childlike, in that regard, with their wide, blank eyes and doll-sized noses. Their lips, though, were thick and banded like a fish, translucent and perpetually puckered. It hadn't taken long for companies to make mermaid-mouthed sex toys. Skyla had browsed them online, for research. Just like on the real thing, the lips on the sex tubes were thick and slippery, forever open.

"Here, give them another," Zania said, digging out another piece of kelp. "They've earned it."

A mermaid launched into the air before Skyla had even fully extended her arm. She thought of the dog they used to have, when she and her husband were first married. It didn't wait for fingers to clear the way before diving for treats.

The mermaid that jumped was a rainbow of red and brown, her nipples the exact shade of rust crusted on sunken submarines. When she opened her arms, tissue-thin fins opened like wings beneath her arms and between her fingers, or, the appendages that were placed in approximately the same location as arms and fingers would be, were she human. Skyla thought of flying squirrels. The mermaids seemed to be able to mirror any animal or person at any given time. They were human-like and ape-like at the same time. They had winged arms, like bats. They were children. They were sex objects. They were mostly mild-mannered vegetarians. Bottom feeders. They were savage ship wreckers. Skyla stared down into the water as a mermaid stared back up at her, both waiting.

"I feel like Narcissus," Skyla said. "Except I can't tell if they are a reflection of women or not."

"They're not," Zania said. "No more than a rhino is your reflection." She tossed a handful of kelp into the water and the mermaids scuffled to get it like seagulls fighting over crumbs.

"Do you think they're as happy here as they would be in the ocean?" Skyla asked.

"They don't know the difference."

"I'm not sure I agree," Skyla said. When she worked in the lab, she could tell the difference in behavior between the dogs in the cages and the dog she went home to pet. One was happy, the others were not. "Does that make me an animal empath?"

"If you want to believe that, sure," Zania said.

"You enjoy a lot more freedom than the average person, in your line of work," Skyla said. "Traveling, no Monday morning meetings. What's that like?"

"Every life has its limitations," Zania said. "I'm free in my own way. I'm not in others. When I'm ready to retire, I'd like to go back to Florida."

"Will the mermaids be freed when they're too old to perform?"

Zania shrugged. "These are the first generation of trained mermaids. We'll see how they do."

"You mean how long they last?" Skyla asked. She felt a pang of pity for the mermaids. It had to be boring, swimming circles over and over in that tank. Where was the sand for them to burrow? The kelp for them to hide in? Open water to be free in? Maybe she was crossing over to Gwyn's side.

Skyla fished a piece of kelp out of the bucket and held it over the tank as the mermaids still squabbled for the shreds of what the queen had tossed in. A mermaid darted out of the water, biting Skyla's hand as it wrenched the kelp free.

"Ow!" Skyla yanked her hand back. Blood beaded along the bite mark. She knew she'd get a bruise where the mermaid's jaws clamped shut on her skin.

"Have to watch for that," Zania said. "They're all about food. Survival instinct."

"Do you have disinfectant?"

Zania laughed. "Come here."

Skyla followed Zania down the steps toward the back of the tent. She threw open a flap and they walked out onto the back lot of the circus. Trucks and trailers were packed in neat rows overlooking the sea.

"Is there a bathroom back here?" Skyla asked.

Zania opened the door to a trailer and went in, leaving the door open. She came back out with a large wire square, like a collapsed tomato cage.

"I'm going to sell a few of the trained mermaids to other zoos and aquariums," Zania said. "Little side hustle. I need to catch some more. Let me show you."

"Is that a trap?"

"My own design," Zania said. "Come on." She walked off the edge of the smooth asphalt, ambling her way over the rocks toward the water.

Skyla watched after her, unsure of her footwear and the algae-slick rocks and what the woman hobbling over boulders with a trap the size of a folded-up card table was doing. Skyla followed.

Zania got to the edge of the water and waited for Skyla to catch up.

"Low tide," she said, handing the cage to Skyla. "Pop it open."

Skyla pulled up the sides of the cage, the top popping into place with a series of hooks.

"We don't have bait," she said.

Zania plucked clams from a tide pool. "This isn't their first choice. But, it'll do. She set them inside and loosened the blue fisherman's rope that had been twined around the back of the cage. "I like to anchor it with rocks. If you use anything else too man made, they'll notice. Usually, I take the time to camouflage the cage with kelp, but this is for demonstrative purposes." She rearranged rocks to prop up the cage, then buried the rope under the heaviest boulders she could lift. "Get those over there," she instructed.

"You think you'll catch one?" Skyla asked, heaving rocks on top of the rope.

"I think you might catch one," Zania said, winking. "It's a great arm workout, isn't it?"

"How many more do you have to catch?" Skyla dropped a rock on the rope.

"Three? Four?" Zania stepped back and wiped her hands. "Not bad."

"When will you check on it?"

"Low tide, early tomorrow," she said. "You'll be here?"

Skyla surveyed the white caps on the ocean miles from where she stood. Barges and fishing boats floated slowly back into the bay. Skyla had forgotten about the recording on her phone. Tomorrow was Sunday. Skyla flipped the trap door into place.

The Legend of Emma Sondheim

Priscilla Kint

Priscilla (she/her) is a Dutch YA writer. She completed the MA Creative Writing at Bath Spa University in 2018 and is currently working on a Young Adult paranormal novel set in the same world as her short story THE LEGEND OF EMMA SONDHEIM.

"I don't think you should go. You know the Circus won't let you."
Lumen walked ahead of me through the room. We were on the
second floor of our building, the only building I'd ever known.
Still, standing here, surrounded by mirrors placed at odd angles,
it felt like I was in a different world.

This room used to be open to visitors. Our Circus, in times long
gone, used to be a walk-through experience. Guests would roam
the hallways, floorboards creaking. They'd find out about the
stories hidden in their tea leaves behind the curtains of Lady
Aubury. They'd watch anything from dance performances to
magic tricks in one of the auditoria. They'd have their try at balancing a tightrope, only to watch a professional at 32 feet move
faultlessly.

But no longer. Not since the Circus had started claiming rooms
for its own.

"How long do you reckon it'll take before the Mirror Room
becomes inaccessible as well?" I asked.

Lumen walked around, their face reflected back at me at least a
dozen times. "I don't know. I just hope you'll be here to witness it."

"That almost sounds like you want this room to fall."

They turned, looking straight at me this time. I'd always admired Lumen's determination and stature. They stood with their shoulders straight, black hair either the finest of curls or braided tightly to their scalp. "No, Emma. And you know very well that that's not what I mean."

I shrugged. I hated goodbyes. Why couldn't Lumen just act like everything was normal? Why couldn't we be best friends, as we had for years? "I wish you weren't mad."

"I wish you'd get out of your lovesick brain for a second to see what you're about to do." The words stung, like rose thorns pressed into my palms. "It's Jeremiah, Em. Do you honestly think you can trust him?"

I stepped away, elbow knocking into glass. "Of course I can. I love him."

"He's also a naïve idiot."

"Lumen!" Normally, I'd slap their arm, laugh it off. But not this time. This time felt more serious. More final. A goodbye was a goodbye, after all, whether I liked it or not. "Don't you see? I have to go. There's nothing left for me here. Someone else can mop the floors and dust the windows from now on."

"You signed the contract. You've always known what that meant. When you join the Circus, it's forever."

"Yeah," I muttered, my hand in my pocket. "Well, forever is a long time."

"And in all that time no one," Lumen said, "And I repeat, *no one* has ever managed to leave the Circus and live." Their lips moved a thousand times around me, each image in perfect synchronicity.

"No one has ever tried. Not really." Those were Jeremiah's

words. And he was right, up to a point. I'd heard of people trying to leave, of the Circus locking the door on them, keeping them inside. But a locked door wouldn't hold anyone who truly wanted to get out.

"Girl," Lumen said, taking me by my wrist and dragging me along. The open doorway began to appear in some of the room's reflections, so I knew we had to be close to the end of this maze. "You know what they say about the Circus, right? It lives. It breathes and it feels and it hits when it needs to. It travels but does not move. It learns and it—"

"It shifts and it hunts to feed itself when it gets hungry," I finished for them. "Yes, I know. Shouldn't that just make you want to leave more? Who wants to be supper for a magical building?"

Lumen shrugged their shoulders, turned a corner, and then we were out. Back in the hallway, everything seemed oddly dark compared to the Mirror Room behind us. A rumble passed through the building, and I closed the door behind us.

"Right," Lumen said. Their voice was lower now. In this place you could never know for sure who was listening in to your conversations. "The way I see it, it's all about balance. The Circus takes what it needs, and then it's satisfied. It *has* you, Emma. It's got all of us. But if you leave..."

I remembered the final line of the mantra, the one that we all said each morning before breakfast. *When the Circus gets hungry, it is insatiable.*

A shiver ran down my spine.

"I'm sure it'll be fine," I told Lumen.

"But what if you're not? Once the Circus jumps, it'll leave you right here, stuck in the timeline like everyone else out there. You'll be all alone with no way to reach us."

That was the catch, wasn't it? Our Circus was a travelling circus, even though it was contained by a building. Once it decided it would go, it left. From one year to another. From the 1900 to the 1790s. From the Golden Age to 2019. That was why we all stayed inside. If we went out, who's to say the Circus wouldn't decide to leave right away?

Jeremiah didn't fear it, that moment when the Circus would take the leap and leave us. He saw it as an opportunity. I had to agree with him. Sometimes it takes leaving something behind to find your way to a better place.

"Please, don't go." Lumen stared at me, eyes shining. So I hugged them. I hugged them close right there and then, standing up on my tiptoes. Their scent was as familiar to me as my own. I tried to save every strand of it, locking it in my memory forever. Lumen smelled like what I imagined trees to smell like. Wild and strong and full of growth. Those were the moments I'd remember them most. Every time I sat under a tree, I'd think of them on the tightrope.

"I'll come back," I told them, my eyes squeezed close. "Once the Circus returns to this year, I'll come back to visit."

***

The year was 1815. My bag was packed. Not quite as heavy as I expected it would be, but not entirely uncomfortable to carry, either. I met Jeremiah in the downstairs corridor. Paintings graced the walls on both sides. Landscapes, mostly. I had a favourite: a view of a dawning sun over a lake. I hoped I'd get to see something like that soon.

"I believe I've packed everything," I announced.

Jeremiah nodded, his short hair springy after a fresh shower. I wanted to tangle my fingers up in it and kiss him—but first things first. "Me too," he said. "Let's get out of here."

Through the wide opening on our right, we could see the main theatre. In the sandy middle, our team of acrobats was practicing. They were dancing around, toes pointed, twirling before a somersault, climbing on top of each other to form complicated figures, nothing but hands and the crooks of elbows to keep them together.

Two green eyes spotted me in the doorway and smiled. It was young Cole, his blonde hair slicked back tightly. I smiled back.

Maybe I'd miss this more than I gave myself credit for. Maybe the Circus had a lot to give, after all. Family, for one. All of these people here, I knew by heart. Each and every one had something special, even if I hated them sometimes.

But outside had so much more to offer. Places that wouldn't be determined by brick walls. Sights that could go on forever. Time that went in a straight line instead of in the loops and the circles the Circus chose for us.

I was tired of being stuck here, tired of being the talentless janitor in a place of magic and dreams come true. So I took Jeremiah's hand, staring at the leather braided band around his wrist. "Yes," I said. "It's time."

We stepped out without saying goodbye. No one but Lumen knew. Anyone else might stop us, Jeremiah had warned me. He was right. Better to rip the bandage clean off.

The front door of the Circus had a big, bronze handle that I turned gingerly. To my surprise, it opened right away. A light breeze of cold air met us on the other side. I breathed it in, laughing. "Oh my gosh, it's letting us go."

Jeremiah walked past me, arms out wide as he stepped onto the street, sunlight on his face. He was shining. "Come feel it, Emma! Come feel freedom!"

I took my bag and followed him outside without looking back. The door behind me closed on its own, its clang announcing the last time the Circus would ever speak to me.

***

Lumen didn't smell like trees, I quickly found. In fact, nothing in this outside world smelled anything like the Circus had done. There was something dusty and dense missing, something that I'd been breathing in for so long that I had thought it the scent of normalcy.

Jeremiah kept laughing all throughout the day, and all throughout the next day and the next and the next. We ran across the city— even though it could barely be called a city at this point in time.

We slept in an inn. As payment, we helped to clean and cooked meals that the owner had never heard of. He was so happy with us after seeing his customers come in for seconds that he told us we were free to come back whenever we wanted.

We walked through every street—every single one but the four surrounding the Circus. The uneven paths felt like clouds to my feet. I couldn't remember ever having worn shoes for such a long time before.

We danced the evenings away. Sometimes in bars with live music, sometimes on the squares, where people would cheer us on and throw copper coins our way. They asked where we learnt to dance like that, said we looked as graceful as the swans flying south.

Perhaps I wasn't as talentless as the Circus had always made me out to me.

"We should do something special tonight," Jeremiah said one day as we sat in the park, the grass tickling our ankles. His face was so close to mine that I could count the freckles on his nose, on his forehead. I reached forward and kissed each one.

"Like what?"

"We could leave town? Move on to the next one?" The playful look in his eyes set my heart right on fire. Then his arm slid around my waist and my skin began to bathe in flames as well. "I want to see the entire world with you."

Of course, I told him yes.

***

There, on that village's main square in 1815, we stood with our bags packed once again. My pale green dress was brown at the edges, coated in bits of dirt and earth. I liked the look of it and twirled. This dress would see the world, I thought. This dress would get to dance countless times.

I took Jeremiah's hand and squeezed it. He looked so handsome in his linen shirt, his collar up and a long-tailed coat trailing behind him when he walked. "Can we go south?" I asked him. "Like the swans?"

"We can go anywhere we like," he said, and planted another kiss on my lips.

There were several others in the square: married couples walking arm in arm, a group of young boys in breeches chasing each other. An evening like every other for all of them. For me, it was the beginning of something new.

But then the ground trembled. My feet felt unsure and I looked up at Jeremiah. His frown told me that he'd felt it, too. No one else seemed to, however. The boys kept on playing and the couples kept on walking.

The tremble returned, worsening until we were both shaking. Shocked, I let go of Jeremiah, all my attention aimed at keeping my feet steady. I tried to look across the square—surely now everyone else felt it too?—but couldn't. Everything was hazy, as if covered by a thick mist. There was the corner of the pastor's house, the clattering sign above the bakery and—a bus stop.

"Jeremiah," I said, pulling at his coat. "Do you see that?" I pointed, blinking in an attempt to make the mist go away.

The bus stop flickered in and out of view, electric lighting showing some commercial for a new ethical shampoo blend.

"Oh god," I said, my throat dry. "I think the Circus is travelling. Is that what we're seeing? The world changing around us across time?" I looked back at Jeremiah. He was staring ahead, his eyes perfectly still, looking grey through the mist.

"Jer—"

I stopped, touching his coat once again. It was hard and ice cold, as if carved out of stone. My hand trailed up, fingers rough against his arm, his shoulder, his cheek. All of it was the same. Hard and cold. His eyes stared ahead without a pupil in sight. His hair was made up of hard, immovable lines. The leather bracelet on his wrist seemed to have become part of his skin. And all of him, grey. Like stone. Like a statue.

I stepped back, my breath hitching as I saw his feet and his suitcase, both rooted to the stone of the square as if they'd been there forever.

When the Circus gets hungry, it is insatiable.

Quickly, I checked my arms, pulling the sleeves of my dress up frantically, looking for patches of that same grey devouring me. There wasn't a single one.

Jeremiah stood right in front of me, feet hip width apart, one of his hand outstretched as if to grab mine. His mouth was open just slightly. I could imagine him saying my name. *Emma. Emma. Emma.*

Not a sound came out of him.

If any passers-by cared to notice, they'd see a woman in a minty dress with her arms around a statue that none of them could remember having been there before. They'd hear her wailing, calling out for a man who could no longer hear her. They'd see how she clambered back up eventually and started running, leaving her suitcase next to an almost identical stone one.

I saw it all happen as if that woman was someone else, detached as I was from my own body. All I knew is that I had to get help. I had to find someone who understood, who could bring Jeremiah back to me. So I ran through the streets that I'd danced on just hours before, straight back to the Circus. Once it came into view, I allowed myself to breathe. Everything would go back to normal if I just went through that door and let someone help me. Lumen would help me. The ringleader would help me.

I knocked on the door, but no one opened.

"No. Come on, Lumen. Open up. *Open up.*" I started slamming the door, my fist colliding hard with the old wood, its hinges creaking. I slammed and slammed until my eyes fell on the side of the building. I saw the shattered windows, the grey remnants of what had once been curtains.

Fear began to gobble me up as I reached for the doorknob. I touched it, and the door swung right open.

Inside, everything was coated in dust. No furniture. No paintings. No Circus. All of it gone, off to a future I would never reach.

I stumbled back, my vision going in and out of focus. Alone. I was alone. Trapped in a time I didn't know with my family over a hundred year away and my beloved motionless in the middle of a square.

Slowly, the strength seeped out of my legs. I sunk to the cobblestones. My cloak was thrown back by the wind, so I took it and wrapped myself up in it. Then I lay down and let the tears slip free.

***

"She went mad," the man in the armchair said.

The Circus was moving around him, the room filled with a whole new generation of performers. The contortionist stretched herself on the couch. The ringleader stood by the fireplace. The young trapeze artists sat huddled in a corner.

"That's what happens when you try to leave. If the Circus decides to travel on without you, you either turn to stone or become frozen in time, destined to roam an empty world for the rest of eternity until you go mad." The man smiled. "Just like Emma Sondheim."

The room was silent save for the cracking of the burning wood in the fireplace.

"Some say she's still walking about outside to this very day, trying to find a way back."

The ringleader clicked her tongue. "You do like your ghost stories, don't you, Charley?"

"Legends," Charley clarified, swinging his legs down from the arm of his chair. They landed on the carpet with a soft thud. "It's a legend, but it's real. They lived right here, under this roof. It was all real. Excuse me, Penelope," he said, looking at the scoffing ringleader. "You don't believe me? You live in a time-travelling building with doors that scream the moment you touch them, and still you find this hard to believe?"

The trapeze girls moved from their place on the floor. "Is it really true?" the youngest, a blonde girl wearing a soft pink skirt, said.

"It's just a story. It didn't actually happen," her older sister answered.

Charley merely shrugged his shoulders

The girl stared around the room, her blue eyes big as saucers. "But we still won't leave the Circus, right?" she asked.

"No," the sister replied, closely watching the adults in the room. "We'll never leave." Though, somewhere, deep inside her heart, the tendrils of a desire had already begun to grow.

The Harvest-Bringers

Natasha Grodzinski

Natasha Grodzinski's work has previously appeared in From Arthur's Seat and Three Drops in a Cauldron. She currently lives in Toronto, where her main past times include discovering increasingly creative ways to store books in a city-size apartment and going for long, wandering walks in the woods.

Time flows in unfathomable ways at summer's end.

Thea had felt the high sun on the back of her neck, sweat at her temple, the daylight breeze across her flushed cheeks, and then she had turned away, to drift, to dream, to become a lost princess at the side of a stream, and in the moments while her attention was elsewhere the sun danced, dipped, and disappeared. Another rich September sunset. The most beautiful warning there is to mark the passing of time.

She startles at the rich gold on the horizon, her foot sliding down a slick stone and landing in the cold water of the stream. She swears—quietly, as though Mama is waiting in the bushes to catch her out, employing a favorite curse of Papa's that he often mutters under his breath whenever it rains, or it snows, or his swinging axe is not strong enough to break the Black Forest wood.

There's no time to shake out her wet boot, to let her stocking dry in the last stretches of light, or to bid a final farewell to the kingdom she had created at the side of the stream. There is only encroaching darkness and the nightmare of Mama, a mountain in the kitchen doorway, wooden spoon held tightly in a fist, face pinched like a crow's beak. It always begins with, *Where have you been, Dorothea?* Then, *Did you pick the juniper berries like*

I asked? Then, *You see, Josef? You see what happens when you let this child roam free?*

And Papa always says, *Marta*...pleadingly, consolingly, while Thea watches shadows pass over her feet.

There's no helping it. Thea cannot pass a stream without planting stories at its edges, cannot walk past a great pine without perking an ear for faeries, cannot crawl under juniper branches without glancing over her shoulder for gnomes. Papa says it's because the *Waldmeister* spirit lives in her, just as it lives in him.

Thea loses no momentum at the hill, the final crest before she reaches the valley the farmhouse sits neatly within. She pushes up, and onward, digging her heels into soft grass and keeping her eyes fixed on the peak of the hill. As long as Thea has been alive, she has always seen the hill as the border between the forest and the world outside of it. The dream and the waking from it. Thea usually dreads it, the return to the house and to her chores, but now, with the fingers of night curling over her shoulders, she lets out a sigh of relief.

Almost there.

Thea is watching the approach of that peak so carefully, so determinedly, that she does not watch the ground under her feet.

Anyone who walks the woods will tell you this is a mistake. Some think the secrets of the forest play out in the swaying of branches against the sky, and some think they can be found in the call of one bird to another, but the truth of it is, a forest holds all of its stories in the ground: in the scuttle of a beetle across a leaf, in the scent of moss on a log, in the roots that burrow deep beneath the surface.

Thea does not yet know of this world underfoot. She does not watch, and so, she does not see where deep green grass has given way to dark mud, a gift from the last rainstorm that roared down from the mountains.

Her heel lands, strong and sure, and then slides, and her heart sinks low —rolls into the bottom of her stomach when her leg gives way, followed by her torso, her head, and finally her flailing arms.

She shrieks, a cry that echoes into the valley as she falls, hands clutching desperately at the air. But there is nothing she can hold, nothing that can stop the momentum that now drags her down, heels over hands over head, nothing that waits for her at the base of the hill aside from a heavy landing and the ever-watchful pines.

***

She wakes with a pounding head and groaning ribs. Slowly and carefully, she sits up, one hand pressed to the earth, the other holding her aching side.

Around her, the night hisses.

The sun has gone, and instead there is the pale light of a full, round moon filtering through the thin branches of the trees. It sits high, that moon. Too high for it to be early in the night. The air, which had still held the gentle warmth of summer's end at sunset, is now frosty and sharp. Panic churns in Thea's heart.

"How long?" she whispers to herself. Her throbbing head drops into her hands, her knees fold up to her elbows. She makes a toadstool of distress and nauseating fear. *How long?*

She thinks of Mama, pacing by the kitchen door, furious and worried. She thinks of Papa, lacing his boots and reassuring Mama that he is going to find her.

Because surely they must be looking for her now. Surely they must have known where she went. Surely they must be close now, because Thea was at the edge of the valley, the last of the forest at her heels, she was right there—

Her breath catches in her throat.

She had turned in the midst of her thoughts, seeking the place from which she fell, but where she had expected to see the smooth curve of the hill, there is only pine.

"What—" she whispers, rising to shaking legs. She closes her eyes and counts to ten, thinking that it is just the darkness tricking her mind, and that when she opens them, she will see the gap in the trees. She will see the way home.

Yet when she opens them, there is just the same flat darkness of the forest.

I am lost, she thinks, a truth both terrifying and exhilarating. She almost laughs.

There is little that children like her are more warned against than wandering into the woods at night and losing their way. Thea knows the tale of the brother and sister with their bread crumbs, knows of a witch in a house of sweets, and a wolf that pretends not to be a wolf. There are other stories, too, of children being led into the deepest parts of the forest by a kind woman with a sweet voice, of fairies that play tricks, turning day into night and north into south.

Thea knows these stories as well as she knows Papa's smile and the taste of Mama's bread. But she also knows that if she were one of these stories, or if she were the child listening intently with the covers pulled to their chin, she would want to see herself find her own way home. She would want her to be the hero. The hunter.

"You are not a coward, Dorothea," she tells herself grandly. She brushes the dirt away from her dress; stands as tall as she possibly can. "You are the *Waldmeister*."

She squints up at the moon and stars and tries to remember every lesson Papa ever taught her about navigation, but she lowers her gaze back down with nothing gleaned. There's no new guiding sign revealed to her, no direction the moonlight can point her towards, no parting of the trees to reveal a well-worn path.

"Right," Thea whispers, staring down the night that breathes before her. She gathers her skirts into fists and tilts her chin up. "This way," she says, hoping that she sounds more confident to the forest than she feels. "I am going this way," she repeats, a declaration to her surroundings as much as it is to her own feet, which finally pick up, carrying her forward into the trees and the dark.

***

Her confidence falters as she walks.

The reach of the trees is far, and shadows bend and tumble before her like ghosts. Every rustle in the branches makes her consider turning back to where she had woken from her fall. Except now, she's not even sure if she could return there. If she were to turn around, would she be able to find it again? Would she know when to stop walking?

She had given up counting her steps after she reached forty-two. She doesn't know how much time has passed since then. Whenever she glances upwards, she can glimpse the moon, still fixed high above her. Neither falling nor rising.

Doubt is often a familiar gateway to fear, but not for Thea, who was raised in the forest. Thea, who forages and tracks and seeks adventure in the wild. Fear is new to her, and she feels it like stones in her shoes. Over and over again, she whispers to herself, *I am going this way. I am finding my way home. I am the Waldmeister.*

And when even those murmurs of comfort are lost to her, spilled out of her cold hands somewhere over a quiet stream, she finds something else to hold onto: one truth, and one lie.

"I am Dorothea," she says aloud, just bolder than a whisper, "and I am not afraid."

The hope is the lie will become true if she says it enough.

She's opening her mouth to say it again, clenching her fists at her sides for strength, when she notices something in the corner of her eye, the shadows shifting around a small shape. Her voice comes out in a strangled cry, her hands flying up to defend herself from *what* she does not know—perhaps it's a scavenging animal, or perhaps it's a faerie that's been following Thea this entire time, altering her path and blurring the lines of the trees to keep her lost.

This is it, Thea thinks, resignation heavy in her bones, *I am about to become a story.*

She watches, rooted to the ground, as the shape moves swiftly and silently across the forest floor. She has to squint to keep it in her line of sight, eyes straining against the black, until it turns abruptly, emerging from the opaque darkness into a sliver of moonlight cresting over a fallen tree.

Pointed ears and a tail like a brush. A coat that's been washed pale in the dim, but would be a vivid, burnt orange in the daylight.

"Oh," Thea says, and she lets out a short laugh. Then her breath leaves her in one long, relieved exhale. "Hello there."

The red fox pauses on the fallen tree, seating itself at the base where thick roots were ripped from the ground, splaying out like hundreds of tiny fingers reaching back for their home. The fox's tail brushes over the tree's bark. It stares at Thea with blank consideration.

She grins. "I don't suppose you could show me how to get back to the valley, could you?"

The fox cocks its head at her.

"No?" Thea plants her hands on her hips and widens her stance, something she's seen Papa do countless times when describing how he faced down an elk, or a badger, and Mama do countless times when facing down other villagers at the market.

The fox just continues to stare at her.

Thea sighs. "Fine." There was a part of her, small and childish still, half-expecting that the fox would begin to talk, just like in a fairy tale. "If you can't help me, then I'll be going," she says, but when she takes one step forward, the fox suddenly moves, leaping down from the fallen tree and padding away, its body slipping between a thin gap in the pines.

Thea doesn't hesitate before following it.

"Are you leading me home?" she whispers, pushing a branch away from her face. She can just see the fox's tail bobbing in front of her. "Or are you leading me further away?"

The fox glances back at her, as though to make sure she's still following before it continues on, leading Thea out of the trees and into a clearing where moonlight pours down in bucketfuls. It softens the world to a dream. Thea gasps at the sight of it.

The fox sits beside her, folding its tail over its paws once again. It meets Thea's gaze when she glances down.

"Is this your home?" she asks, gesturing towards the clearing. A giggle bubbles out of her—born from her own silliness, at the strangeness of this night and encounter, at the odd wonder of it all. "Do you live here with the fairies?"

If the fox was going to reply to her, it doesn't get the chance to, because just as she poses the question, Thea hears something. She strains her ear towards it, frowning. At first, it's too much of a contrast for her to focus on, the sudden presence of *noise* so startling when compared to the murmurings of a nighttime forest. But as it grows closer, she finds the name for it.

Music.

There's a fiddle and an accordion, playing a tune that would be welcome in a country dance, usually accompanied by stomping feet and swirling skirts. Music, of course, means other people. Other people mean that Thea may have stumbled across rescuers who can guide her home.

She looks down, triumphant, to the fox, but is met with smooth, untrodden grass. She hadn't even noticed that it left her.

The relief that Thea felt at the realization that there are nighttime travelers in this forest is soured at a sliver of doubt that prods at her, warnings from Papa and Mama echoing in her ears: that the forest sees so many people travel through it, and some of those people, particularly those who move under the cloak of night, can be dangerous.

Thea gulps. What if she doesn't encounter gnomes or fairies, but criminals? Thieves? Vagabonds?

She drops behind a nightshade shrub, rising up onto her knees so she can peer through a gap in the branches. *You will wait,* she tells herself, willing her racing heart to slow, lest every creature in the clearing hear the way it thuds and thumps. *If they seem... trustworthy, respectable, you will ask them to help you get home.* She nods to herself, like this is the most logical course of action she could possibly take, like this is what the hero of the story would do, and she sets in to wait.

Only a handful of seconds fall around her before she sees it: a wild boar, impossibly huge and imposing, parting the thick grass with its hooves like water. Thea recoils, her eyes wide as they take in its gleaming tusks. On the boar's back sits a woman, wrapped in a golden cloak and with long, dark hair falling down her back like a rippling stream. Her left hand holds a staff, the wood dark and intricately carved, and what Thea thinks might be a sun sitting at the top of it. The woman is beautiful, the very image of a queen, but Thea's eyes do not stay trained on her for long, for just behind her is a procession of travelers, and each of them is just as strange, striking, and fantastical.

There is a man walking behind the woman on the boar, wearing furs and holding another wooden staff. His hair and beard are long, both tied into thick braids. An owl sits on his shoulder, entirely still except for yellow eyes that flit across the clearing. Thea thinks she sees them pause on her shrub for a moment, and she curls down over her legs, closing her eyes tightly and holding her breath. She waits one second, then another, but already is desperate to look again and see what else is coming, to see what else travels through the forest at night.

She exhales slowly and raises her head.

Behind the man with the owl, there is another woman, sitting atop a horse without a saddle or reins. Thea recognizes the horse's color, its short neck and broad hooves—a *Schwarzwälder Kaltblut*. When Thea was very young, she saw one hauling harvested crops from the fields to the village.

The horse and the woman share the same flaxen hair, the woman's tied into two braids that reach past her feet. Her dress is strange, made of layers of pale woven fabric that almost resemble wheat, but move and fold with her like cotton. She holds no staff, but has a leather bag tied at her hip.

Merchants? Thea wonders, but she dismisses the thought as soon as it comes. The designation doesn't fit the grand, elegant woman at the front of the party, nor does it fit the young men (or rather, Thea thinks at first they are men, but the longer she looks at them the more unsure she grows) who are now entering the clearing. They spin in circles and leap into the air like birds, their arms stretched out, their deep purple cloaks fanning out behind them. They move at an exhausting pace, but they don't seem to tire, continuously smiling at one another, and cheering when a different song begins before the last one has even finished.

The source of the music is just behind them: two young women playing instruments on a horse-drawn cart, both of them laughing and nodding at an older woman seated next to them, who claps in time to their song. The cart is piled high with trunks on their other side, well-made in beautiful colors, but also well-worn, as though they've been opened and closed so many times their locks are more of a suggestion than a practicality.

It's these trunks—alongside the sight of at least a dozen more dancers (some appearing to be even younger than Thea), a short-haired woman wearing riding clothes with a falcon resting on her arm, and an unnervingly tall man in a wide-brimmed hat leading one of the largest horses she's ever seen—that first draw the word out of her head. *Zirkus.*

It was Sofia Meyer from the village who first told Thea about it, after she travelled to Frankfurt to visit her distant family.

There's a tent, she had said, while her rapt audience, Thea included, listened. *And inside the tent, there are horses dressed more finely than anyone in this village. There are men and women who can fly through the air. There are women who tell the future. There is more than any of you can imagine.*

The description had seized Thea with a rush of wonder, and since that moment, she had wanted nothing more than to be able to venture into one of those tents herself, and to see impossible things.

It fits this procession before her perfectly. Thea cannot imagine what other reason there could be for such a group of people to be together, passing through the woods at night. *A performing troupe,* she thinks with a thrill, *a Zirkus that has come to the Black Forest.*

She nearly laughs when she imagines how envious Sofia Meyer will be when Thea tells her that she got to see the performers before anyone else. She eyes one of the larger trunks on the cart, wondering if one of them is stuffed full of canvas. She wonders where this troupe will finally end their journey; when they will decide to set up their tent and invite people in.

"Hello there," a soft voice says, and Thea lets out a sharp gasp, falling onto her back from her crouched position. Her head snaps up, and there, sitting between her feet, is the red fox. Just behind the fox is a young woman wearing a cloak colored a green so deep it's nearly black.

"You," Thea hisses at the fox, her cheeks flushing with the shame of being caught watching.

The fox cocks its head. The woman raises an eyebrow.

"So you do know each other."

Thea stares up at the woman. She is startlingly beautiful, just like the woman on the boar, but also entirely different from her. She smiles, quick and teasing, and for a moment, under the sheen of the moonlight, she looks just like the fox: the same bright orange color in her hair, the same deep amber eyes.

"He told me," the woman says conversationally, "that he found a stray in the woods. A lost lamb." Her voice is so soft and low that Thea can barely hear it over the music.

"You speak to it?" Thea asks, unsure of what else to say.

The woman reaches down, scratching the fox on its head. "Oh, yes. August and I tell each other everything." She glances back up at Thea, and she winks. "He says you have a curious heart. He likes that about people."

Thea wants to believe this woman with the desperation of the dreamer—that she can understand what a fox wishes to say and speak to it in turn, but there's something in the woman's expression, in her teasing smile, that convinces Thea she's making fun of her.

She pushes herself up from the ground, brushing leaves and dirt away from her dress. The woman is taller than Thea thought she was, taller even than Papa. "I'm not a child," she mutters, focusing on picking at a spot of mud on her sleeve. "I know that animals can't talk."

"Hm. But you are," the woman says. She crouches down so she

can meet Thea's eyes. "It's a wonderful thing to be." She plucks a berry from the nightshade shrub and rolls it between two fingers. "There is such adventure in every moment. Each day is a new story. Each turn you take on a walk could bring you to another world." She pops the berry into her mouth. "Or to the faeries."

"Are you trying to convince me that you're fairies?" Thea frowns, glancing past the woman's shoulder to the rest of the troupe. They haven't paid them any mind. Either they haven't noticed this woman stopping to speak to Thea, or they're ignoring it. "It won't work. I know what you are."

The woman raises one pale eyebrow. "Really?"

"You're part of a *Zirkus*." Thea leans forward. "And you're on your way to set up your tent somewhere for a performance. I've heard all about people like you."

The woman's right hand scratches at the fox's ears absently. She mouths the word to herself, *Zirkus*, and also glances over to the procession, watching them for a moment. When she looks back at Thea, her eyes are bright.

"A performance," she says at length. She rests her elbow on her bent knee, propping her chin up on her palm. "There is one already happening, dear."

Thea squints at her. "Where?"

"All around you." The woman's eyes drift over to the trees, up to the sky, and slowly come down again. "You feel it, when it all begins to change, don't you?" She lifts her right hand from the fox's ears, holding her open palm up. "Summer wanes. The sun tires and the nights grow longer." The hand folds down, then turns over, and opens back up so her palm faces the sky. "The Earth sprouts its wares for harvest. The leaves burst into color before they wither. Everything changes, you see? It's a dance all around you, no, a *Zirkus* as you say, every act being performed to perfection."

"I don't understand," Thea says. The woman's words are soft and lulling. They roll over her like a bedtime story, as simultaneously comforting and disquieting as every fairytale she knows.

The woman's smile is patient; indulgent. "When you see these things, these miracles that mark time, it is because of us."

Thea's gaze returns to the troupe. She can only see the woman's back now, the one who sits atop the boar, but if she looks at her out of the corner of her eye, it looks like there are stars in her hair.

"We change the season when we are called to do so," the woman continues. "Take time and turn it over. Make it anew."

One of the dancers passes by an old, knotted beech, a memory from another face of the forest. Thea watches as the dancer brushes a hand over it; presses a kiss to the tree's bark. When the dancer parts from it, a wind blows by them that makes the tree bow and bend, and when it rights itself again, some of its leaves have begun to turn red.

"It is thankless, sometimes." The woman sighs. "There are no great songs of us, or curious tales. But we know how to make our own fun." She laughs, and it sounds like rustling leaves.

It's impossible, what Thea is seeing. Beyond a canvas tent, beyond a story. It's *magic*.

"How?" she asks, voice faint with disbelief. She turns back to the woman, and she cries out sharply at what she sees, stumbling back on her heels.

The sleeves of the woman's robe have fallen down to her elbows, and there, on her forearms, there are flowers blooming from the skin. Deep red and violet asters, unfurling towards the night sky, then curling back up, withering in seconds only to be born again. It's horrifying and beautiful to watch.

"What are you?" Thea whispers. Hot tears form at the corners of her eyes, fear and confusion melting together like one pool of burning wax.

"Performers," the woman says softly. Her forehead creases in delicate concern, as though she can't understand why Thea is upset. "Just like you said."

"I don't—" Thea shakes her head. "I don't understand." Is this woman a fairy? A ghost? A forest-dwelling spirit? Is she real? Is she a figment from a dream?

"We can show you," the woman tells her gently. She sounds so much like Mama, coaxing Thea to come back inside when she has been out for too long, and at once, all Thea wants is to see her, to have her come up behind this terrifying, wondrous woman, wielding her wooden spoon with a scowl. "Come, Dorothea," the woman says. She slowly reaches one hand out, an aster blooming from her wrist and curling into her palm. "Come, and you'll see. There are wonders all around you that you cannot begin to imagine." Her hand halts between them, waiting. "Would you like to see the world, Dorothea? As it really is?"

The thought, *How does she know my name?* is so fleeting in Thea's mind that she barely even registers it, too overwhelmed with her churning feelings of fear, confusion, and —most alarmingly —excitement.

Despite every lesson every story tries to tell, despite every warning from Mama and Papa, she thinks about taking the woman's hand. She thinks about being welcomed into the fold of the troupe. Would she sit on the cart, with the musicians? Would she spin with the dancers? Would she ride on a wild boar? Would she walk alongside a fox? A badger? A deer? Would she be able to touch a tree and turn it to autumn gold?

Magic, the very idea of it, is almost too intoxicating to refuse.

Almost.

"No," Thea says quietly, picturing Mama and Papa, their farmhouse, their animals, her room, her small collection of books, a pot of fresh stew on the table. "No," she repeats, more firmly. "I don't want that."

The woman's face falls, just for a moment, and she returns to her full height, letting out a low sigh.

"If you're certain." She says it like a warning, as though Thea will be disappointed when she realizes what she has done.

"I am." Thea's voice cracks on the second word.

The woman lifts one shoulder. "Then you better get going, Dorothea." Her eyes flick to the front of the procession. "Before they notice."

Thea takes one step back, then another.

"Take care, dear." The woman waves a hand at her, a small violet aster curling around her thumb, before she turns away, pulling the hood of her cloak up. The fox glances back at Thea, revealing nothing in its sharp gaze, and then it follows the woman, weaving between the gaps in her steps.

Thea spares one more moment, just one more, where she watches the dance and absorbs the song of the troupe, and she pictures herself amongst them, just once more, before she turns on her heels and flees into the trees.

***

She runs without thought of direction, pushing aside twigs and branches and leaping over stray roots and pools of mud. It's as though the forest is working with her now, urging her onwards in the way the wind pushes at her back, in how the moonlight seems to be lighting every place she's about to step.

She runs until her chest is burning, until she isn't sure that she can run anymore, and that's the moment she bursts from the line of trees and finds herself at the base of the hill that leads to the valley.

This time she takes it at a walk, carefully watching her steps. When she reaches the top, the familiar sight of the farmhouse is enough to bring tears to her eyes again. She sniffs, rubbing at her nose with her mud-caked hand.

Home.

She tears down the hill at a run, letting out a small cry as her momentum carries her all the way to the front door.

She's expecting Mama to be furious and relieved when she enters the house, to run to her and hug her, to tell her that Papa has been looking for her all night because they were so worried. But when she closes the door behind her, it's to see Mama in the kitchen, placing a pot on the table.

"There you are," she huffs when she sees Thea, wiping her hands on her apron. "How many times have we told you to come home *at* sundown, Dorothea, not *after* it?"

Thea's brows furrow together. "I—" she starts, not even sure what she's going to say, but Mama holds up a hand to stop her.

"I don't want it to happen again." At Thea's dubious nod, she waves her off. "Alright, then. Dinner is ready and your father will be home soon, so go clean up. You're *covered* in mud."

Thea walks to the back of the house numbly, as though she's passing through a dream. *How long?* she wonders. *How long was I gone?*

It's the cuckoo clock in the main room, a beautifully carved wood piece that mama had to trade a great deal of wool for, that tells her. The smaller needle points to the inscription for seven, the larger hand pointing to the six.

Seven-thirty.

Thea was sure she had been in the woods for *hours*, possibly even all night. But this...it's as though she had fallen down the hill, then immediately rose and made her way back home.

It's as though it never happened.

***

"Dorothea! Bring that here!"

Thea grunts as she lifts the basket of potatoes out of the cart, swaying with its weight as she carries it over to Mama and the market stall they've taken for the day.

"We're already late," Mama sighs, gripping onto the lip of the basket and dragging it towards her. "If your father hadn't—" She ends the thought before she can finish it, rolling her eyes to the gray sky. "Gather the rest of it, quickly. I want to get something sold before the rain comes."

Thea leaves without a word, returning to the cart for the next basket of potatoes.

Since Papa was injured in a hunting accident in the spring, she and Mama have been frequenting the market more than usual, peddling produce and wool, trading and selling until the sun goes down. All summer it has been this, Thea hauling baskets—from the farmhouse, to the cart, to the table, back to the cart—and giving half-smiles while Mama chats with the other villagers, a never-ending line of gossip and bargaining. Thea will daydream of the bubbling stream at the edge of the forest while Mama laughs at a snide comment from Frau Krüger, will long for the books in her room while Mama subtly nudges her in the ribs and raises her eyebrows at Henrik Schneider, who, in the last few years, has grown like a tree and widened like a bear.

A summer of this, lacking naps in the sun and adventures in the forest and everything Thea has long associated with the warm months at the farmhouse. Now, the light narrows and the nights grow cold, but the neighboring wheat and corn fields are bursting, and Mama sends Thea to help them for payment. A summer of this—departing early for the fields in Papa's coat and falling asleep at dusk still wearing her boots. Her hands are raw and her eyes are hollow, but if she ever complains to Mama, she receives the same response:

You are no longer a child, Thea. You know what our situation is. You know that your father can no longer work the forest like he used to. We must all do our part. If you wish to stop working, then marry the Schneider boy. Now that family —oh that family —could take care of us all.

Thea barely knows Henrik Schneider, has only ever spoken to him a few times, and whenever she does, she's reminded all over again of why she tries to avoid him.

Her *Bollenhut* slips down her forehead, covering her eyes. She swears under her breath, nudging it back up with a closed fist. She hates that hat. She hates her long, exhausting days. She hates having to speak to Henrik Schneider. She hates that, ever since she turned nineteen, Mama talks about little else aside from the fact that Thea's stubbornness towards marriage will make her a burden to her parents, and she will be forced to live out her final days old, alone, and poor.

But when Thea thinks of her life, lines up the coming years like rows of stalks, she can see nothing apart from this: her long, exhausting days and the constant reminder that the best thing a young woman in the village can be is married. She has considered cutting her hair, packing a bag for the hunter's camps, and pretending that Papa had a son instead of a daughter. She has considered fleeing to Frankfurt, to Munich, and seeking any kind of employment there. Yet as little as Thea knows of the cities, of anything apart from the farmhouse and the forest, she knows that the world waits for young women like her. It waits for them to stumble, nervous and eager, into its depths, and it waits for them to make a mistake. Then it swallows them whole.

So, no. Thea does not do any of these things, because she is afraid. Afraid to run, afraid to stay, left with one foot in dreams and one in resignation.

She shifts the basket into her arms and a potato rolls out, bouncing down the cart and onto the ground, rolling into the bustle of villagers dancing from stall to stall.

Thea swears again, not bothering to lower her voice and not caring when it causes an older man at a carpentry stall to frown deeply at her. She follows the potato's trail, weaving around the bodies she passes, and she marvels at the fact that it's still rolling, despite how even the ground is here. It's as though it has somewhere to be. It's as though it is leading her somewhere.

The thought is embarrassingly whimsical and childish, and Thea admonishes herself for it. *You haven't thought that way since—*

This is the moment she notices the fox.

She stops mid-stride, her mouth dropping open in a silent gasp. Someone knocks into her from behind, grumbling about young women and their need to disrupt *everything*, and Thea steps aside to let them pass. Her heart is pounding, her eyes searching out another glimpse of that bright orange tail in the blur of black, brown, and green. She catches it ducking behind a barrel and she surges forward, gathering her skirts up in her hands. She knows she must look mad, chasing an animal through a market, but she cares little for what anyone else will think. She *knows* that fox. She is certain.

It's the one from her dream.

That is what she has told herself it was for the last ten years: a dream, brought on by the injury to her head from her fall. For so long, it has been the only possible explanation.

Yet now, Thea is chasing down that dream while she's wide awake, in the middle of a bustling crowd, and she's sure that it is him. August. That's what she said his name was. *August.*

She skids to a halt next to the barrel, panting, and her heart falls when she doesn't find the fox there. She turns, her heart in her throat, desperate to find something that will tell her the very thing she's wanted to believe all these years: that it wasn't a dream. That that night in the forest, Thea saw something— something too impossible to imagine.

She lowers her eyes, seeking out small paws amongst human feet, but what they discover is the edge of a dress brushing against the ground, a dress colored in a green so deep it is almost black. Thea's eyes travel up the back of the dress to the place where it's met by a long braid of red hair. Fox red.

Thea can't breathe. There's wind in her veins. There's a fiddle playing in her chest.

The sleeves of the woman's dress are long, and when she moves, Thea can see that she's wearing gloves.

Thea has no name to call, nothing but the dream of a girl singing under her skin, but it's as though she can hear her anyway, for her head turns, amber eyes drifting over the crowd before they stop, resting on Thea.

And she smiles.

The Circus and the Library

Melodie Corrigall

Melodie Corrigall is an eclectic Canadian writer whose work has appeared in The Short Humour Site, Halfway Down the Stairs, Bethlehem Writers Roundtable, Corner Bar Magazine, Blue Lake Review, S/tick, Subtle Fiction, Blank Spaces, Toasted Cheese, and The Write Place at the Write Time (Check out www.melodiecorrigall.com).

When the circus married the library, she was only a small fair. Once the nuptials were performed, however, audience demands increased.

The circus, always stumbling to satisfy, expanded and diversified. With frantic compliance, she added more and more acts.

Although frightened of heights, the circus was compelled to include a trapeze act. Clothed in a scanty, sequined costume, the terrified creature minced her way across the wide expanse. She dared not suggest a regulation safety net, instructed as she had been to keep expenses down. Below, the crowd oohed and awed, warning her to take care while threatening disfavor if she lost her nerve.

She was the pretty girl (such a sweet face), the one in the satin outfit who held the torch when the magician did his tricks. It was she who caught the scarves when he was finished, picked up the rabbit and the hat. When he threw the knives, cavalier in the knowledge that a slip would not cut his throat, it was she who trembled expectantly.

The library, medium-sized when the couple married, expanded at his convenience. No smell of sawdust, no sweat of crowds, and no greasepaint or animal droppings for him. Defined as he was in books, the library was civilized. He recorded history. "Silence please, people are reading." No animals here, only order, blessed order, and time for all things.

At night, the library closed. The lights were turned off to preserve energy; the shutters were drawn. The staff nodded farewells and filed out, smiling. The library slept.

Not so, the circus. It was in the evenings that the largest crowds gathered and shouted for more.

They waited expectantly for the lion tamer to be eaten, the trapeze artist to fall, and the fire-eater to be inflamed. And even after they finally lumbered out, dropping popcorn and drink containers, leaving to return to their real world, the circus continued. Alone now, without an audience and no encouraging applause, she struggled on: cleaning, packing up, feeding the animals, and mending the broken bones.

The library was the library, open or closed. The books, breathing a life of their own, needed no one to affirm their worth. They waited, confident and uncaring. The circus depended on the crowd, waited expectantly to see the audience's mood. Fearful that something would go wrong, a bad review, a poor gate, an unplanned-for disaster.

Whispers: "The circus will close down."

The aging circus, paint peeling from her coloured wagons, her canvas rent, struggled to keep up the show, adding more and more unlikely attractions.

Scheduling was difficult. The audience careless of the animal's health, the staff's fatigue, demanded more action. What are we paying for? Might as well stay home and look at T.V. Bring on the lions.

The circus didn't tame the lions herself; she was too timid. She only entered the cages after the show to clean the cages.

In time, to satisfy demand, the circus bloated her thin frame into a balloon-like fat lady. Comments from her fans and from the media confirmed that she was grotesque. They call it as they see it. Keep them coming, keep them laughing.

One February, the circus wound down; the music limped from 7/8 to 3/4 time. In a retrospective moment, the circus confessed to her seated companion that she took wanted to be in the book business. The library was too wise to concern himself with such carnival fantasies. "A circus is a circus," he fondly offered. Then to her strident barks, "Keep your voice down, you will disturb the books."

When the circus married the library, she was only a small fair. When they separated, she transformed into a ship and sailed away.

To the Pole!™

Lisa Gregoire

Lisa Gregoire writes fiction and faction
from her home in Ottawa.

When my alarm dingled, I left the gift shop front cash to Jeanette, walked across the bridge that connects the iceberg and the propeller vessel, took my seat in the front row and started pedalling with the rest—university students, Maritimers, Inuit—all of us young and carelessly fit in our It all goes South from here!™ shirts. The sky was huge and royal blue, but swirling wind made it feel cooler than what the thermometer read: 14°C. The crowd was puny, fewer than 20. The cruise ship from which they'd come was moored a kilometre away. A few pasty guests were circling the mammoth vessel on jet-skis and stand-up paddle boards, like anxious exiles.

Folks love the pedalling part. My parents could have installed mechanical jets from the get-go to move the iceberg into place every day. But where's the drama in that? my dad would ask. Where's the high-viz, low-carbon emissions messaging, mi amigo? You can't do that with a brochure! Like many things up here, it was a mirage. Other than propulsion, everything was powered by an underwater gas generator. Don't ask, my dad would say. Don't tell.

The iceberg, a white-painted, mostly oblong floating theme park called To the Pole!™, was made of steel and aluminum, about 150 metres across one way and 100 the other. Arctic nations were each allowed one such craft at the North Pole, and my parents had an exclusive licence for the next 15 years. It was a gold mine.

True to its nature, most of the structure was under water—offices, food storage and prep, animal units, bathrooms. Above sea level, the surface was open and flat to accommodate visitors who usually congregated near the snack bar, which sold hotdogs and multi-flavoured "iceberg" sundaes, or the gift shop, which was crowded with polar bear pillowcases and Arctic tchotchkes made by people in warm, impoverished countries. In the centre of the structure was a three-storey tall cylinder of baffled fabric painted with aurora borealis. It swelled pleasingly in the breeze.

We pedallers smiled and waved to the visitors' phone-blocked faces and their bored, overfed spawn. They waved back with non-dominant hands, leaning hips into safety railings, careful not to drop expensive devices into the Arctic Ocean. They all wore wide-brimmed sun hats and baggy, blaze-orange To the Pole™ flotation suits. A chubby pylon army.

The Russians totally copied us but then took it up a notch. Instead of pedallers, trained rowers, ripped like doped-up medalists, moved their iceberg around. We were cutesy and painfully Canadian but it polled well on feedback surveys. At that moment, the Russians were stroke...stroke...stroking away from the pole because it was our turn. I spied Svetlana, third row middle, long brown hair in a messy bun and lean, tanned pipes. "Hey!" I yelled. "Prekrasnaya devushka!" When she blew me a kiss, I closed my eyes and inhaled the smell of salty seaweed and her sweat.

Faisal burst through a slit in the tall curtains dressed in a top hat, jodhpurs and boots. He'd told me about the ringleader costume over drinks the night before and he was right: it totally worked. He'd been Santa Claus for a while but people found the

Christmas thing confusing. Before that, he was an Inuk hunter with sealskin smock and pants but the Inuit Federation threatened to pull our licence if he didn't cease and desist.

"Ladieeeeees and gentlemeeen, welcome to the top of the world!" Faisal bellowed, his amplified voice overloud for a small crowd. "Thank you for joining us. Soon, hearty adventurers, you will arrive at a sacred place. Today you will make it To The Pole™!" The pylons whooped and applauded.

"As our human-powered propellers draw us toward our destination—thank you pedallers, on behalf of the environment!—let me introduce you to some of our Arctic friends. First up...Tuuga, the unicorn of the sea!"

Tuuga the narwhal. Last week someone asked about the brown patches on his skin so now he's further away, his tusk rainbow painted for distraction, and Tytoosie is out narwhal hunting again. A narwhal's tusk is porous and sends messages to its brain about water chemistry and temperature. Svetlana told me so. She's studying to be a biologist. I'm not studying anything, apart from Svetlana and my dad's accounting files, but still. Painting the tusk seemed unwise and also ridiculous.

Tuuga pierced the water's surface with his clown tusk, and visitors cheered. At my mother's command—she was head trainer—he breached and splashed and speared plastic rings tossed by some rich kid who won a contest. Kid had a good arm for once. The last ring was attached to a silk rope and when Tuuga swam away, the rope tugged a lever and fireworks exploded overhead, mostly invisible in the glare of polar summer sun. People were dazzled, but people are easily dazzled when fire and noise are involved.

After his performance, Tuuga swam wearily to a herring pellet dispenser inside a foam igloo before retreating to the area behind the kitchen where staff sometimes toss old French fries. Visitors always ask why the whales don't swim away. We tell them it's training and food that keep them close, which is sort of true. There's an electric fence that zaps them when they try to swim beyond it. The animals learn pretty quickly how far they can go, so it only hurts for a short while as they're getting used to it. That's the training part.

"Thank you Chonglin," Faisal said, patting the ring-thrower on the back. "You want a job?" The kid giggled, covering his mouth with his hand. "And now, my friends, say hello to Betty and Barney belugaaaaa!"

Mom says belugas are easy to train. She gets them to jump and twist and splash. Then they swim alongside the berg and spray the crowd with their quirky blowhole sphincters. As usual, visitors squealed with delight that day. When the whales posed and chirped for the money shot, Esther flipped on the snow machine and ice crystals filled the air, melting on the crowd's upturned, well-moisturized faces. I convinced dad to buy the machine last year. I told him the North Pole needs snow. I'm good with stuff like that.

At mom's signal, Barney and Betty hastened to the food igloo then, phantom-like, faded into the indigo depths. It felt like they couldn't wait to get away from us. I didn't blame them. I wanted to escape sometimes too.

Belugas and narwhals are the sole members of the monodontidae family, Svetlana says. Fraternal whale twins: one white and stuffed-animal cute, one stippled grey, mysterious and armed. I went through an Arctic phase when I was a kid and got stuck there. That polar yin-yang of delight and danger proved intoxicating. I wanted to be Knud Rasmussen, travelling across the

Canadian Arctic by dog team, visiting Inuit clans, navigating by horizon lines and patterns on snow. Amundsen, Frobisher, Franklin—all of them moustachioed and blundering about for thrills and fame, their Inuit guides amused, skeptical, probably pitying. For outsiders like me, the Arctic has always been an amusement park, and now that it's warmer, even more so. That particular day's small crowd notwithstanding, business was booming.

"Aren't they something?" Faisal shouted. "Fun fact: beluga skin, with its layer of vitamin-rich fat, is an Inuit delicacy."

"Ewww," visitors scowled.

"We're getting close," Faisal teased. "In just a few..." A wind gust sent his top hat tumbling across the fake ice surface and towards onlookers. A woman thrust her foot sharply right like a football goalie and stopped the hat cold. The crowd went wild. Faisal stood momentarily frozen, like a hatless Frosty the Snowman, and waited for the applause to subside. Then he sliced his hands through the air and shouted, "No goal!"

"Ha-ha-ha," people laughed, myself included. What a ham.

"Get on with it!" some redheaded kid yelled.

Faisal retrieved his hat, bowed deeply to the insolent punk and then swept his arm skyward as though unsheathing a sword. After an awkward but brief delay—Esther missed her cue—a giant screen unrolled to show our fluctuating GPS coordinates. I checked my monitor: N 89° 99' 41.78".

Our destination, at N 90°, was the Geographic North Pole, a fixed point at the top of Earth's axis. Magnetic North was totally different, a fugitive creeping steadily from Canada, where it once resided, to Russia. Maybe Russia was reeling it in, like Svetlana had done to me The two Norths, like the monodontidae, were also twins: one predictable overachiever, one shifty delinquent. I didn't blame Magnetic for running away. Her brother had become something of a shill for trinkets and cheap spectacle. But it wasn't his fault. It's all he'd ever known.

"Arctic explorers before us trudged and skied and sometimes perished crossing vast expanses of ice to reach the pole," Faisal said, bending deeply and shuffling toward an imaginary blizzard, falling to his knees, crawling. An aspiring actor, he loved this part. "Now, we can reach this remote area on the open sea!" Here, he held his arms aloft, triumphant. On the big screen, the longitude tracker spun like a slot machine as we approached the pole, the centre of the circle where all lines of longitude begin and end.

Visitors gaped silently, perhaps puzzled by the numbers or else distracted by Faisal's melodrama. He rose slowly, milking it, then shook his finger at the screen. "We're almost there, intrepid mates! While we wait, let's meet a few more northern residents."

Esther cued the circus music and four ringed seals waddled out from under the giant curtain wearing branded pillbox hats on offer at the gift shop. Their trainer, my twin sister June, followed behind in a sparkly bodysuit and long blonde braids. She betrayed no hint of a hangover despite the endless whisky shots she'd done with Faisal and me the night before. Our evening's sloppy conclusion was hazy but I remembered her declaring repeatedly that she was so done with this place. "How could you turn your back on easy money," I slurred around midnight, feigning disbelief. What I meant was: How can you leave me behind?

The seals nosed multicoloured balls back and forth to each other as they undulated through a figure eight formation, arf-arfing and slap-slapping their front flippers on the metal surface. Up came the face-eating phones. Tap, tap, tap.

"Another fun fact: animal rights activists temporarily destroyed the Arctic economy and a generation of subsistence hunters late last century because they decided seals were too cute to eat," Faisal said, pausing and nodding to the crowd before delivering the zinger. "Imagine how cows felt!"

"Ha-ha-ha," people laughed.

"Thank you, June," Faisal winked. Those two were always flirting. June curtsied, cleavage offered, before parting the curtains for the seals and disappearing. "Don't forget to sample our new seal burgers at the concession!" he said. People grimaced. I told dad they would be a hard sell but he didn't listen. "Our next entertainer loves seals too...but not because they're cute. Aaay-Ohhhh...Nanuuuuuq!" he howled, sounding like a wrestling announcer.

A Viking in a plastic chest plate, horned cap, and ratty fake beard emerged from behind the curtain holding a big chain attached to a polar bear. Geoff, the Viking, was recently promoted from dishwasher to bear handler because of his bulging deltoids and square, Norse jaw.

Visitors gasped and took a few steps back. Nanuq was thin, slow-moving and groggy. His eyes were ringed red and his right hip was balding where he'd been rubbing against his cage. He swung his heavy, flat head back and forth like a pendulum, stopping periodically to sniff the air. Nanuq was one of the last legal polar bears in captivity, grandfathered until he died, which always seemed imminent. His death would be a huge loss. Erasing him from the promo materials alone—and designing new ones—would take weeks.

"Vikings were the first explorers to trade with Arctic peoples," Geoff said out of nowhere, going off script. Faisal raised an eyebrow but nobody was listening anyway. They were transfixed. "Say hello to Nanuq, King of the Arctic!" Geoff said, cracking his whip. Nanuq reared up onto his hind legs and roared, wheeling his front paws lazily as though swatting flies and then falling back down to all fours with a thump.

"He looks drunk!" the redheaded brat yelled, and he lunged at the bear with his arms in the air.

Then a bunch of things happened.

The bear roared and swiped at the kid with a massive paw, catching and tearing the fabric of his survival suit with a claw. The kid screamed. His parents screamed. Everyone else screamed, and ran, but there's nowhere to run really, except to the perimeter railing. Geoff zapped Nanuq's electric collar with a remote control which left the animal swaying and bawling like a human child. Then Geoff unholstered a tranquilizer device and pressed it to the bear's neck. Nanuq opened his mouth wide, in either a yawn or a lazy snarl, and exposed an armoury of sharp, yellow teeth before laying his chin between his front paws like a dog and passing out. My dad, who must have been watching on screen from his desk, suddenly appeared with a medic. They lead the boy and his parents to our office behind the snack bar.

"No need to fear. Nanuq will be dreaming for hours," Faisal said, a little too buoyantly, I thought. He turned up the corners of Nanuq's mouth in a smile to prove his point. "A helpful reminder of why it's important to follow the safety rules outlined in the waiver, am I right?" Visitors whispered and pulled their children closer. Great, I thought. Another early morning debrief from my dad tomorrow about risks and best practices.

I checked the GPS and realized we'd drifted away from the pole. Faisal caught my eye and wound his hands in reverse but we were already back-pedalling. We only had an hour before the Norwegians came knocking, and time was ticking down. With Viking Geoff standing beside Nanuq like a proud hunter, Faisal beckoned the reluctant crowd to come closer for the finale.

"We are seconds from reaching 90° North latitude. Watch the screen and count down with me. Ten...nine...eight..." Staff passed out plastic flutes of champagne to the adults and grape juice to the kids, and I tethered the pedal craft to a shared floating dock at the pole to hold us fast. Then I walked across the little bridge to the iceberg to shoot videos for the website.

When the countdown expired, Faisal declared our arrival, pulled a rope, and the curtain fluttered down to reveal our giant pole, white with a red swirl like a candy cane. Faisal raised our To The Pole!™ flag, Ode to Joy blared out of the speakers, and confetti canons blasted their corn-based, biodegradable ammo.

Reaction from the still-stricken crowd was muted. Some visitors tried to applaud but couldn't because they were holding phones and champagne so they just murmured praise, hugged hesitantly and took pictures of themselves with forced grins. The music faded out at the two-minute mark leaving nothing but quiet chatter and the gentle lapping of waves. A pod of orcas appeared outside the containment field and I held my breath as they passed, their shiny black skin glistening in the sun like wet liquorice. Sometimes, when I can't sleep because of the infernal sunlight, I imagine swimming with orcas, holding their dorsal fins as they skim the surface of the sea and plunging with them into the cold, viscous ocean.

"It's just a stupid pole!" yelled the redheaded kid, yanking me out of my reverie. He'd been miraculously revived with a deep fried pogo and blue slush drink. We all turned to him and his parents.

I'd never admit it to my dad but, well, the kid had a point. It was just a pole. But it was our pole and it would eventually be my pole. When I allowed myself such fantasies, I imagined Svetlana and I taking over the business. Maybe June would be there to help run it. Maybe we'd set the animals free and make it more science-y and educational. You know, or not.

Unfazed by the remark, Faisal smiled his way over to the boy and knelt down to meet him eye to eye.

"Darn," he sighed, producing a gaudy golden badge from an inside pocket. "And I was just about to make you Arctic Ambassador."

"I wanna be the 'bassador!" the boy cried, looking up to his parents and then back at Faisal.

"Well, you have to believe in the magic and promote this sacred place," he said gravely.

"I will! I will!"

"That's my boy!" said the father. Faisal pinned the badge on the kid's orange suit.

"Well, that's our show for today," he said, rising with a flourish. "Thank you for being our guests at the North Pole. Be sure to tell your friends about us." He shot me a brief, stricken glance, as though, given the bear attack, he probably should have skipped that last part, but it was too late.

The redheaded ambassador and his parents approached Nanuq for a photo. The kid posed, giving the bear the finger. His parents laughed and laughed. Then a girl of about ten went up to Nanuq and gently combed his fur with pale fingers as a tear ran down her cheek.

"Don't worry," Faisal said, placing a hand on her back. "He's just sleeping. He'll wake up later."

"I know," she said. "That's why I'm sad."

***

After our allotted time at the pole was done, we pedalled back to our corporate dock as the Norwegians slid soundlessly into place with their sleek, solar and wind-powered iceberg. I didn't care for it. Too post-modern.

Our guests climbed into a couple Zodiacs and returned to the cruise ship with their free Arctic Explorer Certificates, and staff set to work shutting down for the day—retracting the pole and screen and transferring Nanuq back to her undersea pen with an industrial forklift. I grabbed a broom and helped sweep up popcorn and plastic and then attached the garbage bins to drones for mainland disposal. When everything was locked up, I took a water taxi back to the International Polar Station where we all stayed in summer, alongside scientists and research nerds. I sat at the back of the boat and stared at the churning wake where manufactured waves collided with natural ones in a bubbling tumult.

I met Svetlana at the bar. We ordered chicken wings and took our vodkas to an outdoor table on the deck.

"How'd your day go?" she asked.

"Some kid got whacked by the bear."

"Holy shit. Is he OK?"

"Oh yeah. We plied him with junk food and made him ambassador."

"No, Nanuq!"

"Oh, ha-ha. Yeah, he's fine," I lied.

Svetlana unclasped her bun and her brown hair tumbled down around her shoulders. She ran her fingers through it like a shampoo model. It's hard not to be aroused by such exotic beauty. Hard to resist the desire to possess it. The sun loitered on the horizon like a relentless surveilling eye. She sipped her drink and frowned. "Needs more ice."

The Dog and Pony Show

Piper

Piper is a brain scientist, a circus aerialist,
and loves horses.

Magic is what happens when reality breaks. That was always true, and a special joy of the circus has always been to see that happen, or almost happen; close enough to feel like magic. It's what people came to see—tigers turned tame and people flying free of gravity's relentless pull. Danger, too—the tiger's teeth and the negative space of the fall.

When reality broke everywhere (let's say *shattered* instead; there were deep cracks and missing spaces, along with chunks that remained relatively intact) that felt like magic to me too, tremendous and uncontained. I'm no authority; I don't argue with people who say it was physics, or weaponry, or God.

But it reminded me of the circus. Suddenly we were all ten feet of the ground without a net. (Gravity stayed real and not everyone survived, I know to my own grief—please allow me the metaphor?) The reality-broken world was dangerous, with so many structures and safeguards failing, and so many people failed to manage themselves or cope or be kind in their new circumstances.

I had practiced circus arts for years, though never to the point of performance. I loved the feeling of wrapping myself in silk or rope, spinning and stretching and hanging upside down, and like anyone who puts on a red nose, clowning opened my heart. I was never strong or expressive or graceful, as artists go; I did it for fun, and that was all right. At the time these arts were available to anyone with a little time and money, at least in cities— there were aerial classes at community centers and clowning at old folks' homes. You didn't have to be born to it, and you didn't need to get good. I showed up a few times a week and paid for my classes and that's probably ninety per cent of anything ever, anyway. Circus had been my refuge, and it became my bridge.

Ermine, founder of the school where I practiced, sent out a vast group message — I was on a lot of lists, and telecommunications worked for awhile. I had a horse farm at the time, in a small backyard way, and I was able to ride to a kind of rescue. I hitched Stjarni and Sweetie to my biggest cart, the one for schoolchildren's farm days and the occasional fancy wedding, packed up the ponies' medications and my own, and drove to the studio. The building was intact, as was the bulk of the equipment. People huddled together inside, deciding what to do and with whom.

Everybody wanted to pet the ponies, which they appreciated, and there was much discussion of where I could go and who wanted to go with me. I ended up with four passengers—my teachers Ermine and Tsuto, plus Bett who was a painter as well as an aerialist, and Phil who was a juggler, a welder, and a rigger—and a lot of circus gear. The loaded cart was tremendously heavy, but the ponies did what I asked. We escaped the city without trouble, I think because horses always inspire goodwill even in the worst circumstances, and because the cart's enormous wheels could handle very damaged roads.

Five days and maybe a hundred miles later, we were as safe as anyone could expect to be. The ponies munched grass at what had been a roadside, and Phil set up a fifteen-foot silks rig. We played on it, all of us, just to make ourselves feel good—the height and flight, the suspension and the drop. It felt like trust, and I for one needed that like air. What it looked like—I don't know what I looked like, and it didn't matter. Ermine embodied the sinuous, silky little animal of their name; Tsuto moved like lightning; Phil and Bett flew like a pair of eagles. We were a circus, for small but high values of that old word, and we could use an audience.

I brought my ponies and I've also got a loud voice. So the next day I rode around yelling and finding people—there were people were camped up and down that road for miles. I invited any and all, and twenty-one people showed up. I gave pony rides to start, and then the rest of us performed. Somebody with solar power played a Cirque du Soleil recording for a soundtrack, which I found beautiful and bitter by turns. I wasn't sure we were going to be paid—we would have performed just for joy, as we had practiced. But we were given generous applause, and also food and water, soap and a big woolen blanket. Late that night I asked Ermine, "Was this your plan? Because it was a great one," but they only laughed and told me to go to sleep. I wasn't sleeping well—I never have—but it warmed my heart to hear.

So a tiny traveling circus is what we became. People seemed to like seeing us; maybe we were a safe space for them too, setting them at ease with an old kind of magic. I painted "Circus of Tenacious Joy" in blue letters on the cart, and Bett got us the Beatles' "Yellow Submarine" album and a player, so that was our soundtrack. We didn't have much, either for ourselves or as a show, as the history of circuses went. But most people didn't, and we were a pleasant novelty in a difficult time. We never stayed anywhere more than one night. The arts seem like a luxury at the best of times, and none of us wanted to stand up before much scrutiny either. My ponies were strong—they were Icelandics, bred tough for war or food or any need in circumstances much more dire than what we faced. We kept going.

We took smallish roads, mostly southwest. That was Ermine and Phil's decision; my job was to drive, not navigate. Sometimes when we'd stop the cart I'd ride ahead, and do my yelling if I found a town or a camp of refugees. Depending on the distance and their mood we'd either drive up later or I'd bring them back, a circus parade in reverse, for the show. If I'd led them, I climbed on horseback and escorted them back afterwards, carrying a burning torch for people to see. I had a little speech I gave, usually to final applause and sometimes a few more gifts or coins. Then I'd quench the light and return to the cart in the dark, trusting the pony's eyes. Often I sang, too, just for myself and the rhythm of our ride.

One such night, under a full moon so bright I could see pretty well myself, I heard a wolf howl. It was high and thin and musical, and music was rare in those days. I opened my mouth and sang back, stopping my song to match the note and the quaver as well as I could with my human throat.

The night was dead silent after that. I felt like an idiot, which is a feeling I'm quite used to, but just then it made me sad. I coughed a little and drank some water. It's possible I'd been hearing "Yellow Submarine" a little much, but this was a different Beatles song, "Norwegian Wood". I'd played it in string quartet, in junior high, but now I sang out again with the words: "I once had a girl / or should I say / she once had me…"

There were no lights back at the circus cart, but it was bright enough for me to read the blue letters, black on silver by the moon. It was a warm night, and I saw everyone's makeshift beds outside as well, and heard Tutso softly snore. I untacked Stjarni and let him go to graze with Sweetie, and then I felt a furry shape leaning up against my legs.

I jumped backwards, tripped, and did a perfect pratfall. I didn't yell because people were sleeping, and that seemed more important than that I had maybe literally led a wolf among us. Were wolves still shy wild animals, or were they magic now, predators out of fairy tales? While I sat there on my butt, the animal lay down. I could make out the shape — wolf or a coyote or a big dog, I'm no authority and besides I know they interbreed — and I could feel the animal's posture, cozying up to me.

I reached out and scratched it behind the ears. The fur was as thick as a pony's mane, but softer. If it could purr, I thought, it would have. We sat together for awhile like that. I would never have said I was lonely in the circus before, with the ponies and the performers and the occasional audiences, but some kind of solitude ebbed away from me in the moonlight, through the warmth in my hands.

At length I noted that the ponies didn't mind, and it was very late. I got to my feet, and said, "Come on," to the animal. A bedroll awaited me, along with an apple and a hard-boiled egg and a bottle of water. I wrapped myself up and ate and drank, and gave the beast half of the egg. Then we curled up together, and I slept as well as I ever have.

Phil found us in the morning. Being Phil, he just sat down and waited for me to wake up, and didn't even ask the question in words. "He's my new dog," I said, when I woke up and figured out I had to say something. "His name's Sebastian."

"He's a girl," said Phil. Sebastian had rolled over for tummy rubs, which Phil was providing.

"Don't get gender prescriptive now," I said, and Phil laughed and got up and walked away. He'd left me another apple and some bread for breakfast, and I heard him telling the story to everybody else as they brewed coffee. They all laughed too, and Sebastian was a part of our troupe then, and nobody in the circus asked me to justify or explain.

The audiences were a different matter. Sebastian was big and strong and healthy, and even with as much slack as people cut us, they sometimes looked askance at our big silver-gray wolf. Their dogs growled or slunk away. Ermine made Sebastian a big gold-and-pink neck ruff with ribbons and pleats, and that helped with the people if not their pets. And someone—not me—persuaded Sebastian to sit beneath the aerial rig during performances, bowing or sitting up or tail-wagging, something like a clown. People loved that, and would sometimes try to pet Sebastian afterwards. The wolf never quite allowed it, arch-backed and smiling in her pink ruff. (I went to using "her" after Phil's observation, though Phil maintained "he", which I think was good manners.) When we reverse-paraded our audience back to their homes, Sebastian would trot by my stirrup all the way.

Often we sang together, in the dark on our way back to the circus. I missed having recordings that weren't "Yellow Submarine", but I guess recorded music was a brief blip on musicality anyway, and while I would have cringed at singing for others I enjoyed it for myself. Sebastian crooned — that's the only word I can think of for it. Wordless, softer than howling, for our ears alone together. She grew quiet as we approached the cart, so I would too, and I felt as much peace as I ever have when we lay down together in the dark.

Then one night, our peace was broken.

We'd performed in a beautiful field all green and golden with the fall. Phil and Ermine had been working on duo handbalancing, and Tutso had to restart the long refrain of "All Together Now" before the two sprang apart, laughing and sweating and bowing to much applause. There were thirty-eight people in the audience — quite a crowd for us — and they gave us a huge picnic basket filled with cheese and cured meats and a few bottles of fizzy hard cider. We weren't far from the farm buildings where the people lived, and I'm sure they would have made it home just fine without my escort. I rode with them because I felt like riding, and I felt like being with them for ten or fifteen minutes longer than the show. There was a half moon high in the clear sky, so I didn't even bring my torch. The people were talking to each other, about our act and their own gossip, and I led them and listened and smiled to myself.

I left them at the big farmhouse porch, cheering and waving goodnight as Sebastian and I returned to the road. Two minutes later I was out of sight in the darkness. I had just started singing — "Eleanor Rigby", of all things — and then I heard hoofbeats, galloping to me.

I shut up and we halted, Stjarni brave and cooperative as always. There were five of them, which struck me as absurd — I was one middle-aged woman on a pony, and they were five on five horses. The one in front held a burning torch, and I saw his face, his wild grin. "Get off," he told me, voice loud to be heard over the crackle of its fire. I sat. "Get off," he said again. "We don't want any trouble."

"This is trouble." Argument always comes easy to me. Someone else laughed and rode me down.

His arms were out, reaching for me like a partner acrobat even as I flinched away. We sidled around, but another rider swung a fist into my face. My eye burned hot and white and my head snapped back with the force of it, and I would have fallen if Stjarni hadn't twisted to keep me on. I clung to his mane with both hands, struggling for balance. Then Sebastian roared from my side and leapt up.

Stjarni reared beside the wolf, striking out with teeth and fore-legs as I hung on — I was mostly a passenger then. They were all so much bigger than us, and I didn't have so much as a whip as a weapon. But I had two animal allies, and I was angry as well as frightened and hurt, and I heard myself scream as we fought back.

One horse bolted away as its rider cursed. Then Sebastian sank teeth into the arm that held the torch, and it fell like a meteor. Dry leaves by the roadside caught fire, and another horse spooked; a man landed hard on the road. Stjarni's broad shoulder smacked a horse in the side, and I reached up to punch the rider's face — that one tried to grab me back, but Stjarni and I stayed together. Stjarni wheeled away, running at the fallen man; he left the road to flee on foot, and I fought my pony to let him go. Then the rest were gone too, an arrhythmic rattling of hoofbeats on the road, leaving only the rustle and spark of leaves aflame.

All this took less time to happen than it's taken me to write. (It has taken me, I admit, some time and effort.) I was shaking. The smell of burning leaves was both acrid and sweet. My throat was full of it, and sore from screaming, and I couldn't seem to catch my breath. Stjarni was excited, prancing; he wanted to run after our attackers, and I wanted to just run, anywhere, away. But I said "Sorya, sorya" and my pony quieted as I asked. When he was still, I got down from his back to look for Sebastian.

There was no wolf. A woman lay at the side of the road, dark in the flickering firelight. She was naked except for a pink-and-gold ruff around her neck, and bleeding from the side of her mouth.

"Sebastian?" What a stupid question, I thought, even as I said the name. I knelt down; I had no water with me, but I dabbed at the blood with my shirt. I was afraid to touch her, and afraid not to, and shaking. I touched her hands, which felt hot; mine were icy cold. I peered into her face and her eyes opened and fixed on mine, wide and gold. Her pupils were even; no concussion, and I felt some relief for that. "Are you all right?"

She rolled away. Stjarni put his head head down by me, and I stroked under his jaw. Minutes passed, and I didn't know what to do but wait. A low voice said, "All right."

I had never been so glad of any words. "Do you want help?" I saw the answering nod, and as Sebastian came to her knees, I was beside her. She was heavy, but I was strong. At length, we got her onto Stjarni's back, and left the fire to burn as I walked beside them back to our cart.

The circus had gone to bed, as usual, and I was just as glad. I helped Sebastian (was that her name? was that the right pronoun?) to dismount, and got water, and untacked Stjarni and let him graze. When I came back, Sebastian had taken off the ruff, crawled into my blankets, and curled up tight.

"Thanks for saving me," I said, because it needed saying.

A rusty laugh replied. "Anytime."

I sat on the ground next to the own bedroll, feeling like an idiot, which as I mentioned was familiar. "Do you want anything? Is there something you need?"

"Could you hold me, like you do?"

My heart broke, or something close to that. "Of course," I said, and took off my boots and lay down. She was much bigger as a person, and it took a little arranging, especially since I was afraid of hurting her. But eventually we lay together in the blankets, both our heads on one pillow, my front to her back. "How's this?

"Good." We were quiet for a while. I had one arm over her middle, and the other curled between us, my hand on her shoulder. She was very warm, and I was less icy; it felt good. "How are you?"

"I'm fine," I said, though my eye still hurt. "Are you going to be okay? Are you going to be a wolf again?" Which struck me as rude and I was embarrassed as I said it, even though it was the most obvious of questions.

"I don't know," came the soft answer, and then even softer, "I hope so."

I kissed her shoulder, as I had so often done to my wolf. I didn't and still don't know how that magic works, only what I'd seen and what she said. I said, "I hope so too," and she sighed. At length adrenaline wore off into exhaustion, and we slept.

When I woke up there was a wolf in my arms, and so there has been every night since. I still call her Sebastian, and I still call her her.

For a long time I was inclined to blame the singing, which is to say I blamed myself. That's an empowering perspective: I did this so that happened, and if I don't, it won't happen again. It also plays into what we're taught about womanhood: you don't go out alone at night, not even with your horse and your dog, and you certainly must not sing.

That is nonsense. It wasn't my fault, or Stjarni's or Sebastian's or the circus's. It's tough to know you're never really safe. But that's what we learn from circus—to be in danger, and sometimes like magic to come through it and stand for applause. These are the things that allow me to go on, to survive and even enjoy: a wolf who is also a woman, and the way it feels to be upside down fifteen feet in the air, and not fall.

The Infinite Circus

Aun-Juli Riddle

Aun-Juli Riddle is a writer and illustrator who lives in Baltimore, Maryland with her partner and trio of cats. She runs an online tea shoppe and enjoys traveling the country to sell her wares and collect souvenir magnets. Her work has recently been published in Glitter + Ashes: Queer Tales of a World That Wouldn't Die.

Find her online at www.aunjuli.art and on Twitter as @aunjuli.

The Ringmaster Time Forgot

Murmurs circle the dark from hushed mouths waiting for the show to begin. They've waited seven years for this show to arrive, and now that it's here—as it's always on time—they can't wait any longer.

But they will wait, and Lyra Lane knows it—waiting makes the show that much better.

From behind the curtains, with her eyes closed, she can feel their energy. It's their delicious energy that makes the magic. She waits for the perfect moment, the crest between excitement and agitation, before she takes a deep breath and steps out into the darkness. In this space, before the audience is aware she's there, as she's standing invisible before them but fully present, she remembers how long she's been doing this. Far longer than any of their first memories, an age more than she'd admit to, hiding from Time and beneath Death's nose.

The lights go on, a spiral of yellow and gold speckles her dark skin. She is the universe, stars and all. The pre-recorded introduction captured on old Earth technology jolts on and issues words from a friend, a mentor, lost to time but not from her memories, shake her from her reverie. The deepness of the voice always resonates in her bones. The tenor of *feeling* in the words. The secret stories behind the words and the love embedded in them. "Welcome to the Infinite Circus! It's my great pleasure to introduce you to your story navigator tonight, Ringmaster Lyra Lane!"

Cheers erupt from the stands, and as their energy swells Lyra breathes it into her lungs and roars with a might few on this side of the galaxy have seen—

"Welcome Friends! Fiends! Folks of Atmos 5, the best station on Ceres, to the most spectacular show in the universe!"

As she takes her next breath, swelling with energy and magic, she looks out to the crowd and searches for them. No one she has ever met, but people she knows intimately. Those who look to the stars to find their stories. Those who are waiting to be swept up and lost in a tide of tales. People like her.

The crowd roars in response, and Lyra looks for the one who will one day take her place. The timeless one who is her mirror—they are also the universe, stars and all.

The Eye of the Universe

Before Flora knows about the world, before she understands loss, before she's plucked up and out of reality to swim in magic with the finest acrobats in the universe, her eyes meet the Ringmaster's. She squeezes her mom's hand as a feeling—like the moment before a great adventure or the twinkling of a possibility—courses through her.

Her mom's smile radiates back at her, illuminated by speckles of stars that are swirling around them. She leans down, her bangs falling into her eyes, and squeezes her hand back.

"This is just how I remember it when I was a kid. And Lyra looks exactly the same!" The excitement in her mom's face, her voice, the warmth of her hand, is a moment. A snapshot. Flora tucks it away, filed between clips of sour school days, soundtracks of the rumble of the quarry and weary of the workers, and stills of her mother's illness.

"Thank you for bringing me," Flora says in her softest voice, for the audience is hushed.

Her mom puts her arm around her. "There's no where I'd rather be and no one I'd rather be with. Being with you is the greatest magic."

As Flora's voice catches in her throat, she suddenly feels weightless. She gives her mom a panicked glance and grabs her hand.

Smiling, her mom only says, "It's beginning."

Flora, her mom, and all of the audience of Atmos 5 all begin to float, and their stadium seats seem to disappear into an endless sea of space. Flora clutches her mom's hand for minutes before letting go, wondering what it's like to actually fly.

And they do. The audience floats, circling the main stage like a school of human space fish, swirling around gently as the acrobats in the center twist and turn and spin. As they dance, a blue light radiates from their center.

Magic. Flora knows that's the only way this could possibly exist.

The spectators float gently around the acrobats, the weightlessness a strange sensation even though they live on a space station. Flora watches a story unfold that tells a tale about a mysterious wanderer who meets Fate.

Flora lets the momentum of the crowd pull her like a calm and gentle tide, and seeing her mom's joy, wonders what it would be like to live forever. She's not sure how or why, but she thinks the Ringmaster could know.

When they leave the Infinite Circus, after the Eye of the Universe, after cotton candy, after holographic animals, after face painting, Flora's mind flutters with wistful thoughts.

Over the years, Flora will forget many things unworthy of remembering and willfully ignore impolite memories that intrude on her feelings.

But not the Infinite Circus. She'll always remember the smell of the Old Earth popcorn, the calm in her mom's eyes, and the feeling of being transported into a tale infinitely more beautiful than reality—especially when that reality, eventually, no longer includes her mother.

The Mysterious Wayfarer

Before Lyra Lane takes a bow in front of the Atmos 5 audience, before she dazzles them with her parting smile, before she steps onto the gigantic robotic leviathan ship, she feels something amiss.

The hunger from the audience seemed greater, and she wonders if she's accomplished what she set out to do—provide them a magical escape—when she can still feel their gnawing appetite at her back. Seven years ago they were vibrant. What could change so much in that small amount of time?

She is more exhausted than she can ever remember, and she thinks maybe Time has seen her and has mentioned her presence to Death. As she pats the metallic leviathan, fondly named Echo, in circus tradition, she tries to leave all of her worries outside the traveling space train.

Despite her attempt, a small shadow climbs aboard with her, full of its own worry and wonder.

It isn't until hours later when she's taking a stroll in the dome of Echo and marveling at how much space there is and how, even after centuries, it still takes her breath away, she encounters the girl, a small thing full of worry and wonder.

"You're a long way from home now," Lyra says to the girl who seems older in memories and younger in spirit. "Won't Atmos 5 miss you?" Lyra knows the answer already, but sometimes when you know something inside of you, it still helps to hear it spoken aloud.

"I don't think so. I don't have any family there anymore." The girl looks up at the stars, and Lyra wonders if the girl feels like the universe could swallow her at any moment too.

"Won't you miss Atmos 5? It's your home." Lyra crouches and sits beside the girl who seems more at home on Echo than Lyra has ever felt.

"Yes." It's all she says.

"Did you see the show?" Lyra asks.

The girl shakes her head. "No...not this time. I saw it when you were here last, though, with my mom. It was wonderful."

Lyra smiles. "Thank you. I suppose you were too busy figuring out how to sneak on our caravan to see the show?"

The girl grins. "I saw the beginning. When you welcomed every-one. It's my favorite part."

This surprises Lyra. "Really? Not The Eye of the Universe where you're floating in the air like stardust?" She gestures widely with her arms as though she is announcing in the stadium. "Or Geraldine's Magical Animal Menagerie?" She conjures her top hat and tips it with a wink. "Or Captain Ocean's Voyage?" She leans forward to look at the girl squarely. "Why?"

"Those are all good shows, but the beginning is the best part. It's the furthest from the end of the show." The girl paused. "Like when you love a story and you read it and you have all that adventure ahead of you? Even when you're at a good part in the story, you know it'll be over one day. But the beginning? That's the moment you know you're okay. That's the moment when you have all of the possibilities ahead of you." The girl sighed. "That's when you don't have to go back to real life."

They sit in silence for a little while, universe-gazing, and Lyra can't help but wonder about the girl. They are the same. Both of them a blazing fire burning over deep layers of grief.

"What's your name?" Lyra asks and takes her hat off.

"Flora."

"Well, Flora, I hope you're ready for a new beginning. As much as I'd like to tell you that I can turn this beast around and take you back, that ship has sailed."

Flora nods.

They sit in silence for a while longer, before Flora speaks.

"Will I be okay?" This isn't the fire speaking, it's the grief, and Lyra reaches for her own.

"Yeah. You're good." Lyra gently puts her top hat on Flora's head.

Lyra doesn't tell Flora about being timeless and wandering the stars and creating more voids by chasing memories she couldn't possibly fill. In that moment, she's just grateful for the quiet company, and finally, the absence of hunger and worry.

The Ghost of Ceres

Nothing has changed on Atmos 5 since Flora left seven years ago. Not the way the air purifier smells gently of flowers Flora has never actually seen. Not the way its inhabitants seem gaunt emotionally. Not the way the stars seem to yell from the distance—"We're out here! There's more! Don't lose hope!"

The Infinite Circus arrives a few days before the show, at Flora's request, but she feels like a stranger in a place where no one remembers a small, sad girl who disappeared seven years ago.

Flora visits all of the places that remind her of her mother and even though she imagined she'd feel haunted by the memories, wandering here and there with little to no interaction with anyone makes *her* feel like the specter. The Ghost of Ceres.

She passes through the bustling diner where she learned about pancakes, the shopping square where she coveted things she couldn't afford, and the edges of the building where her mother taught before she was too sick. She couldn't bring herself to go in. She just hovered and watched and *felt.*

When Flora arrives back at the caravan, she feels a void. Sad? She had wondered—worried—whether she'd suddenly be transported back to fifteen, and if she'd feel as unmoored and empty as the day she left. But she feels largely unchanged, and for some reason, that bothers her, and continues to bother her until she waits for the show to begin.

Flora steps into the darkness.

"Welcome to the Infinite Circus! It's my great pleasure to

introduce you to your story navigator tonight, Ringmaster Flora Future!" Lyra's recorded voice permeates the audience and Flora's heart.

"Will you be okay?" Lyra asks, knowing that loss is never easy. "It's my time."

"Yeah, I'm good." Flora knows that loss is difficult, but life could be infinite in stories—in memories.

"This is really just the beginning," Lyra says, her eyes filled with starlight. *"You're going to be a great Ringmaster."*

"Welcome Friends! Fiends! Folks of Atmos 5, the best station on Ceres, to the most spectacular show in the universe!" Flora steps into the dazzling light. She will help the audience escape, weave stories from her memories, and transport them to worlds they could never dream of. Together, they'll create a new beginning.

Paths of Life and Death

Emma Schmid

Emma Schmid is a fiction writer living in London, Canada. Paths of Life and Death is her first published work.

Rhiannon made her way across the circus ground, her cloak whispering against the dry grass at her feet. It was the height of summer, and although the sun had set, casting the sky in orange and purple, the humidity hung heavy, curling Rhiannon's hair. They had been in the town of Ilya for two weeks, but Rhiannon was still adjusting to the unfamiliar length of her new haircut, a souvenir from their show in Luthor. It was so short now that curls bounced against her cheeks and the nape of her neck, tickling her skin like phantom bugs.

The haircut was a good thing, she knew, despite how she'd acquired it. The circus was moving on soon, and in a few days, Rhiannon's debt to the old man would be paid. She'd slip out that last night, get to the main road. She was hoping to go to Wisterium, or the Redthorn Mountains. Somewhere far away from the capital, out in the middle of nowhere, where no one could recognize her.

Around her, the air crackled with anticipation as the performers readied themselves for the evening performance. Torches lit the path Rhiannon walked, illuminating the way to the big top and casting the outlying tents in mysterious shadows. One had to walk off the path to reach Rhiannon's, the fortune-telling tent, and to meet those other oddities the old man displayed. *In the whole of Carterra,* his posters said, *you've never seen anything so strange!*

And strange they were. The woman with spikes through her skin, a man with an elongated neck. The boy who was raised by wolves, quite literally...and Rhiannon, the one who could see death—though this was not her job at the circus.

Rhiannon watched the shadows of the acrobats and trapeze artists dance across the canvas, their shapes oddly distorted, given too-long arms and legs. They became menacing as they swung and flipped and danced wildly across the tent wall. She heard the cacophony of laughter ringing inside and hurried her steps, veering out of the torch light.

Her tent, pitched right beside the big top, was miniscule, with only three chairs and a table draped in gauzy purple fabric that shimmered in the candlelight. Rhiannon passed her reading table and stood before the large three-faced mirror. Behind her, the candle on the table flickered, casting her veiled face in even more shadow. With a steady hand, she raised the veil, examining the face beneath with heavy resignation.

Rhiannon was lovely—her curls, though shorter than they used to be, were thick and dark, the colour of walnut. They framed a fine-boned face with high cheekbones and warm ochre skin. It was her eyes that ruined the picture.

Before, her eyes had been deep brown, flecked with the slightest bit of green, but after...Rhiannon's eyes glowed like melted bronze, a liquidy gold that gave the illusion that her irises were churning like the sea.

When she was young, after the curse settled in her, her mother told her to always wear the veil, to never look people in the eye.

It was her mantra, the words she whispered to her six-year-old as she brushed her hair, fingers catching in the tangles.

"It will protect you," she would murmur. In the mirror, Rhiannon saw her mother's glassy-eyed reflection—she stared at a spot just above her head, never looking down into her daughter's eyes. She could feel her mother's looming presence now too, like a shadow behind her, the reminder that she *must not* take off the veil.

But Rhiannon had.

***

Luthor was a coastal town made of sharp cliffs and rocky beaches. The wind roared at the rock face; the waves beat at the shore in a deafening rhythm that jostled the fishers' boats. It was a town with old values: family, loyalty, religion. The type of close-knit community that worked together for peace, and joined forces against anything they deemed evil.

It wasn't a particularly rich town, but it had lots of kids, the old man said. They would get money out of the parents. So, the circus came to town.

The first few nights were a delight—the tumblers and trapeze artists awed the crowd with daring tricks, the clowns made laughter echo through the circus—the torch-lit path up to the big top was filled with people queueing for the tent, waiting impatiently to see the heart of the warmth and joy that the circus was so well-known for.

But, in a tent just off the main path, Rhiannon was readying herself for her act. She was the fortune-teller, soothsayer, and every night she prepared the small, contained hearth in the back of her tent with wet wood and leaves. As the smoke filled the tent, shrouding her in mystery and shadow, her patrons listened to what she divined of their futures.

Smoke and mirrors, the lot of it. The only gift of prophecy Rhiannon had was that of death. It was more a curse than a blessing.

Rhiannon examined herself in the gilded mirror as sweet-smelling smoke filled the tent. This was her nightly ritual, the only time she ever took the veil off—when a face appeared over her shoulder.

It was a young boy. His round face was eager, eyes wide with wonder as he took in the smoke-filled tent, the woman shrouded in a deep purple cloak. In the mirror, their eyes met, and the boy went still.

Rhiannon rushed for the veil she'd discarded on the table, knocking over her lantern with a *crash*, extinguishing the light, but it was too late: a shiver ran through Rhiannon's body, and suddenly she was at the coast.

Far away, she could smell the cloying scent of her smoke-filled tent, but salty sea air whipped at her face and cloak. She stood on a rock outcropping, the churning waves hundreds of feet below. Rhiannon turned her face inland, looking for the boy. Every ounce of her pleaded that he would not be here, that perhaps she was having a nightmare, but he was.

Rhiannon had spent many days and night in her tent, teaching herself to recognize the features of her victims so she could pinpoint their paths. The boy's face was still round, his light hair the same length. His death would come in the next few days, then. Weeks, maybe.

In his hands he clutched a kite string. High above them, the beige kite flew through the air, graceful as any sea bird. He grinned as he raced it across the cliff's edge. Rhiannon pressed a hand to her stomach, hoping to staunch the waves of anxiety churning inside her.

It was no use, of course. The sun was nowhere to be found as clouds rolled across the sea, getting darker by the moment, and the boy was having trouble controlling the kite. He tugged at the string, stepping closer to the edge of the cliff as he tried to claw it back.

Rhiannon watched, entranced, as he took another step, his mouth screwed to the side in concentration. *No*, Rhiannon wanted to say. *Stop.*

Rhiannon felt the gust of wind before the boy did—the kite string was ripped from his small hands, and as he leaned forward to catch it, balancing on the tips of his toes, the wind shoved against his back, sending him plummeting for the black water below.

One moment he was there, the next he was not.

Rhiannon turned away.

She blinked into the darkness of her tent, recalling the lantern had fallen over. A headache blossomed at her temples, the familiar after-effect of her visions, but she ignored its aching.

Is the boy still here? She wondered. *Will I be able to warn him?*

There was a sound like ripping fabric, and a single match flared to life in the heart of the tent. As the lantern was re-lit, light filled the room, illuminating the boy's pale face. Rhiannon was never sure what happened to the subjects of her visions while she was ensnared in them, but the boy seemed wary of her, now.

"Come in." The words were a desperate plea, and the boy's

eyes went wide with fear. Rhiannon shook off the disastrous vision, pushing the feeling of foreboding down deep inside her. She smiled sweetly, waving a hand at the boy. "I have much to tell you."

The boy's mouth set in a straight line; his small shoulders squared. He couldn't have been more than twelve, just on the cusp of manhood. Rhiannon wondered whether he would take her advice.

"I have seen something of your future," she said plainly. She didn't bother with the far-away voice and mystic hand gestures. She didn't even bother with putting the veil back on. It was too late now, anyway.

"What have you seen?" The boy's voice was still high and melodic, it had not yet dropped to that of a man. Maybe he *would* listen.

"You must not play by the cliff." Rhiannon warned. The ache in her head intensified. She longed to close her eyes, but the boy looked so confused. "The cliffs are dangerous," she went on urgently, "If you play by them, you will fall over the side."

The boy shook his head. "I'm always careful." His eyes skirted around Rhiannon's gaze; he looked over her shoulder, into the mirror, where his scared reflection stared back at him three-fold.

"Thomas!"

A woman's voice cut through the din of revelers outside the tent. The boy's—

Thomas'—eyes went wide. "My mother—"

Rhiannon nodded. "I know. Listen carefully, though, yes? Do *not* play by the cliffs, Thomas."

The boy nodded, but he would not meet Rhiannon's eyes. Once was enough. More than enough. He raced from the tent without a second glance, just as his name was called a second time, the sound cutting a wound straight into Rhiannon's heart.

Three days later, news reached the circus. Thomas had fallen from the cliff.

The old man came and beat her with his staff. Rhiannon was thankful that he had not used the whip. That thankfulness lasted only until he allowed the mob of Luthor folk into the circus ground, where they dragged Rhiannon to the stocks and cut her hair before locking her in the device. They called her names and threw stones that cut her already bruised skin. They screamed at her, screeching that it was Rhiannon's fault the boy had died. She stayed there for three days.

She felt the weight of her gift grow heavier on her shoulders. They were right. She was not the wind that pushed the boy off the ledge, but she felt like it, in a way. Invisible, powerful... dangerous.

***

Outside Rhiannon's tent in Ilya, the circus was open for business. Despite the mirthful music that promised a good show, the circus was devoid of patrons. Travelling as they did, with caravans and coaches, animals in tow, rumour often travelled faster than they did.

Rumour said that Rhiannon killed a boy back in Luthor.

Although Rhiannon had not actually done the killing, the stain of the crime had sunk into the cracks and crevices of the circus, leeching into the fabric of the tents and blackening the glitz and glitter, staining the very ground the circus was built on.

The old man could feel it settling over his show, his pride and joy, and immediately knew what had caused it. Though blessed with no gifts himself, the old man had a talent for finding those gifts in others and using his cruelty to exploit it. He saw it reflected in Rhiannon's golden eyes when she was just nine years old, eyes that showed death and that other thing the god of death reigned over: riches.

It was easy to take the girl from her mother. The woman was a sickly thing, practically skin and bones. He found it peculiar that she didn't say goodbye to her daughter, hardly even looked at her as the old man dragged her away, paying the woman's miniscule debt in trade for her child.

"She is cursed," the woman spit. She knelt beside the hearth in the small hut they called a home and prayed to the gods for forgiveness. The old man had set up the circus in the next town over, and caught the girl sneaking in without paying admission the day before. She wore a veil, which he tore from her head as he shook her roughly, demanding payment.

The instant he looked into her eyes he felt a distant shiver: someone had walked over his grave. The little girl went rigid in his arms, her gaze far in the future. He wouldn't know her gift until her mother confessed it that day, by the hearth. Still, he didn't ask to hear the details of his death, and Rhiannon was not forthcoming. He put it out of his mind entirely, in fact, until the day he felt the stain of Rhiannon's curse on his circus and vowed to put a stop to her madness.

***

Rhiannon sat calmly at her reading table, awaiting her first customer. The smoke filling the tent added intense pressure to the heat of the summer evening, stifling Rhiannon in her thick cloak. The other performers told her it would add mystery to her performance. In reality, all it did was make Rhiannon sticky with sweat.

At some point in her life, she'd become accustomed to the sights and sounds of the circus—the merry music, the chatter of the crowd, even the noise and stench of the lions and bears: all this was familiar to her. Perhaps the most familiar sound was the heavy gait of the old man as he tore across the circus grounds. No matter how loud the circus was, if he came near Rhiannon, chances were her ears would perk up like a cat, all her senses flaring to catch if he was coming for her.

Today was no different, although the deserted circus made it easier for Rhiannon to hear his clomping footsteps, set against the harsh buzz of the cicadas. The tent flaps were shoved aside, parting the thick smoke.

"This is your doing, isn't it?"

Rhiannon lifted her chin, despite the beating that could come as a result of her stubbornness. "What do you mean?"

The old man flung his arms behind him, out to the empty circus. "You've cursed us," he spit. "No one is coming."

"That is hardly my fault. I warned the boy, like I told you. He fell."

"You as good as killed him." The old man's hand came up swiftly: he took steps across the small space, inches from Rhiannon. She held in a sigh.

Her hands came up: an outsider would expect her to protect her face from the blow, but she lifted the veil, allowing slightly cooler air to wash over her face. Her eyes were the one weapon she had against him, and she used them whenever she could.

The old man went rigid, his hand stalling in the air as their eyes met across the tent. As he shivered, feeling his death without seeing it, the vision flashed in front of Rhiannon's eyes. A dark tent, a sword slick with blood, the figure of a familiar, slim man standing in the candlelight. The vision did not draw her in as it had when she was nine. This was but an after image, something she could flash by.

When the vision passed, she saw the old man's hand was down at his side, fingering the whip at his belt. "Put it back on," he snarled, wariness in his eyes. "You'll curse us all."

Rhiannon let the veil fall over her eyes once more, covering the world in black lace. "As you say."

The old man's lip curled at one side; his face contorted with rage. "Be warned, girl." His words carried the threat, though he stepped back towards the exit. "If your debt wasn't almost paid, I'd kill you now."

Rhiannon knew he spoke the truth. One day, probably soon, he would do it. He would kill her, if she didn't escape first.

***

Word passed around Ilya: the circus had come to town. But this was accompanied by other, more dangerous rumours. People murmured to each other in back-alleys and dark corners: the fortune-teller was a murderer; the circus was ruined...the old man was getting frail in his old age. This rumour had been around since the troupe had visited Luthor, and it was this that inspired Rhiannon's escape.

In the quiet hours just before dawn, two days after the old man's threat, Rhiannon snuck from her tent, cloak wrapped carefully around her to conceal the pack she carried. It was full of the things she treasured: a photo of her long-deceased father, her mother's silver brush, clothes and some money she had stashed away. The veil was over her face as usual.

No one heard her footsteps as she crept across the circus ground. It was a different kind of deserted: the world was quiet, the torches unlit. No one would be coming to visit the circus at this time.

In the days leading up to her escape, Rhiannon expected to be nervous when the time came. The anxious feeling of a new experience had hollowed in her gut the night before, but as she rose and gathered her things, disappearing across the field, all she felt was a sense of bitter-sweet freedom. There was a cost to things like this, and the gods always ensured their debts were paid. The dagger at her waist felt heavy.

Fleeing into the woods of Ilya that would lead her to the main road, Rhiannon looked back at the field of dark tents. She could just see hers from the edge of the woods. If she had ripped down the tent, or set it alight, it might be like she'd never come to the circus at all.

***

In the heart of the circus, the biggest tent was reserved for the ringmaster. He slept on a bed of luxurious furs; his tent extravagantly furnished with silver accents and exotic designs. The old man lay sleeping among these furs, one hand curled around a whiskey bottle. His snores masked the steps of the intruder as he slipped secretly into the ringmaster's tent. A well-burned candle sat by the bed, illuminating the old man's face, casting shadows across the cruel lines and showing the depth of his wrinkles. The intruder's sword was already out, the tip glinting in the dim light.

The intruder raised his weapon, expertly slicing the old man's throat. He was dead before the first drop of blood hit the carpet.

The sword, slick with blood, was sheathed as the intruder ransacked the tent, stuffing money and valuables into this pack. Anything that could be sold for a price, spirited away. The intruder would be rich.

Before he left, he leaned close to the old man's bedside. The candlelight illuminated his face, revealing features that were sharp and young, dark eyes and shoulder-length hair tied with a cord of leather. With a serpent's smile, he blew out the candle.

***

Rhiannon waited by the road, wary of the two horses tied to a post nearby. They were chestnut and palomino, each monstrous, towering above her. She'd never been a fan of horses. She watched as they grazed, heads to the grass, ears flattened by the wind. The night was inky black, and Rhiannon stared into it, trying to ignore the shadows of the forest. She dreaded what might be lurking there—she'd heard stories of Fae, but it was those creatures that *preyed* on the Fae, those that the Fae were scared to speak of...those frightened her.

If she could just get through the next few moments, put some distance between herself and the circus, she would be fine. Maybe she would never be scared of anything ever again.

There was a *crack* in the forest to her left—Rhiannon whirled around, heart racing, one hand ready on the dagger at her waist—but it was just Jonah.

Rhiannon relaxed, though her hand did not move from her belt. It was almost time, then. "Is it done?" she asked in the darkness.

A lantern flared to life. There was a dark smile on Jonah's face, though it didn't reach his eyes. They were black as ink, and empty as a well. She knew from the first time they'd met that he liked pain and death, relished it, even.

He stalked towards her, setting the lantern on a nearby rock. "He's dead," he confirmed. "Would you like to see the proof? I've got the old man's treasure here." He patted the sack. "Or maybe you'd rather see the blood?" His hand settled on the sword at his side, but Rhiannon did not want to see.

"If he's truly dead, let's go." Though she turned her body towards the horses, she knew what was coming. Icy dread chilled her veins.

"I think you're forgetting something." Jonah's hand slammed into the tree behind Rhiannon as he crowded her, pressing her against the bark. She turned her face away as his breath curled against her cheek. She held her breath, torn between two views: watching the scene from the road, and here at the tree, the dagger heavy and hot in her hand.

Jonah ripped the veil from her face, his other hand reaching for the folds of her cloak. As their eyes met, he stilled.

Now.

Before the vision could flash through Rhiannon's mind for a second time, she blinked it away and drew the dagger, using all her strength to sink it into his gut.

Jonah's eyes went wide. He gasped, his strength failing him as he fell forward, catching himself on the tree. Rhiannon slipped out from under his arm as the coppery tang of blood filled the air. He turned his head, the beginnings of a curse on his blood-flecked lips, but as he turned to grab at her, he fell backwards.

His eyes dragged away from the canopy above his head, landing on Rhiannon, hate-filled and angry. She breathed deeply as the adrenaline surged through her; every buzz of the cicadas, every chomp of the horses munching their grass: every sound had the delicate hairs on her arms standing up. Even the stars looked brighter.

Rhiannon leaned over Jonah. His breath came slower now; it was almost the end. The veil gone, she leaned over him to look in his eyes, seeing his confusion, but also that hunger, the underlying glint of savagery that lingered in his soul.

Rhiannon had seen it the day they met, the day she learned it was her or him.

***

She was weak, failing fast as she hung in the stocks for another scorching day. Her lips were beginning to crack, too dry without water, her scalp itched from the sun. The scratches and bruises weren't healing well in the heat: flies landed on her every now and then to taste her blood. For the first day, she shook them off. Now she didn't bother; her back ached from standing hunched, and her legs threatened to buckle. But she stood steady, waiting for the old man to come and collect her.

He'll be back soon, she told herself. But of course, she wasn't sure.

That was when Jonah had come to her. She didn't learn his name until he came to her after dark, appearing in her tent the night after she'd been released. A pair of dark, dusty boots appeared before her.

"Do you want some help?" he asked her, his voice a mockery of kindness.

She'd nodded, unable to speak. Any words she tried would end up as a whimper of pain. They'd taken her veil, so it was a surprise when a hand gripped her shorn hair, tilting her neck in a painful arch. The man stooped down to look in her eyes.

His were dark as night, and in the split second before the vision came to her, she saw the evil that lurked in him, hidden behind a veil similar to her own.

As the vision gripped her, Rhiannon saw a fork in the path before her. She had never seen two versions of the future before, but it seemed the gods had smiled on her, for once in her miserable life, and decided to allow her a choice.

She stood by a roadside, disoriented. The pressing heat had gone, a cool breeze kissed her face as it whisked by. It was pitch black, but not far ahead, Rhiannon watched as a light flared to life in the forest. Nearby, a sign told her to head north for Ilya, or west for Luthor.

"Is it done?" she heard herself ask. The pair exchanged words, but Rhiannon was focused on her other self. This other Rhiannon's hair was short, cut close to her head, but she did not look older. This would be soon. She watched as the man that stood before her in Luthor, the one with the dark eyes, came menacingly towards her, too close. He pressed her to the tree she stood against, and then with a sharp *smack*, knocked her to the ground.

Rhiannon did not care to watch the rest, and turned away, covering her ears. When it was over, the man with the dark eyes left the injured Rhiannon by the roadside, beaten, bloody, and dying. He took a pack with him as he made for the horses, riding down the road and out of sight. Rhiannon watched as she died, alone, unable to even see the stars.

Her death was the first path. Jonah's was the second.

The second time she watched the exchange, Rhiannon paid attention. She heard them speak of the old man, heard this new man say he was dead. He'd killed him. An idea nagged at the back of Rhiannon's mind, but she focused as the man stepped out of the woods. This time, though, Rhiannon watched herself stand straight and steady, a hand on her dagger. When the man came too close, Rhiannon sheathed her knife in his gut, pulling it out in one smooth motion.

Both of these paths flashed in front of her eyes in seconds. As she came back around, with the man's dark eyes before her, his hand still holding her hair, she knew which path she would choose. She offered the man, both her saviour and her enemy, a small, pleading smile. "Please, help me."

***

Rhiannon waited until the light left Jonah's eyes before taking the sack he carried. She took his stolen goods, his dagger and sword, and his cloak, for good measure. When she'd cleaned her dagger on the grass at the roadside, she looked up at the stars.

The gods had decided to show her two paths that day in Luthor: she could either die, alone and afraid, or gather her courage and survive.

Rhiannon had never been outside the circus in the eleven years she'd travelled with it. They went where the old man wanted, when he wanted. She had the vaguest notion of what the continent looked like, but beyond that...Rhiannon had nowhere to go.

Still, she heaved herself into the saddle of the palomino, taking the reins of the other horse, and nudged it into a clop. The night was warm, and Rhiannon relished the breeze on her uncovered face as she started away from the circus that once held her life hostage.

She did not look back.

THANK YOU TO OUR SUPPORTERS

Many thanks to our patrons and supporters, especially:

Anna O'Brien • Cathrin Hagey • Kathryn Parsons
Amber • Natalie Weizenbaum • Johanna Levene

Aidan Long • Anna Evans • Bonnie Warford
D.M. Domosea • Erik DeBill • Felicia O'Sullivan
Frederick Stark • J'nae Spano • Katie Conrad
Kennon Hulett • Martin Cohen • Mollie Morgeson
Salomao Becker • Sarah Jackson
Tory Hoke • Steven • carol shoemake

Ally Shaw • BethOfAus • Brit Hvide • Carly Racklin
Charlotte Nash-Stewart • Dirck de Lint • Emily Anderson
GriffinFire • J. Askew • Jen G • Jocelyn Actual
Karen Anderson • Kristina Saccone • Leslie Anderson
Maria Haskins • Matthew Bennardo • Rochelle B • Sian Jones
Suzanne Thackston • Wanda • Kayla • willowcabins

Want to see your name here? Become a patron!
patreon.com/lunastation

About the Cover Artist

Jessica Jackson is an Animation B.F.A. graduate from Savannah College of Art and Design from Atlanta, Ga. Her family recently moved to a new city in Florida and always find time to enjoy the warm sun. Other than working on commissions her time is spent with her husband, their two toddlers and rescue dog.

You can find more of her work at:

https://www.artstation.com/jas9589

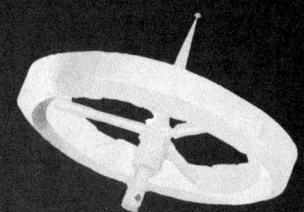

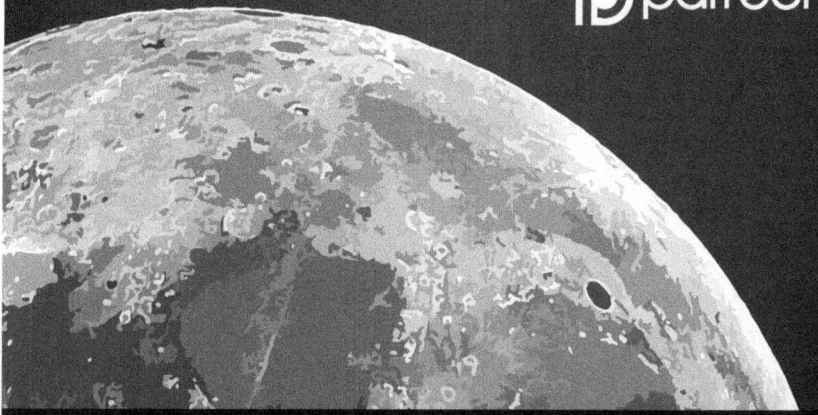